IT TAKES COURAGE TO GROW

THE *Sasquatch* OF JACKSON FARM

A STORY BY

Christine & Christopher Kezelos

The Sasquatch of Jackson Farm

ISBN-13: 978-0-9984628-6-8

Cover art by George Evangelista

zealouscreative.com

First Edition
Printed in the U.S.A

This book is dedicated to anyone who feels unseen and unheard.

May you find your voice.

May you find who you are in all your colors and all your shades.

May you find where it is you belong, your place, your home.

May you find your people.

The kind of people who won't clip your wings.

Whose hearts will fill with joy when they look up and watch you soar.

Seed

CHAPTER 1
Second Chance

The Trinity River flows for many miles through the meadows, forests, and canyons of northwest California just below the Oregon border. It pushes its way deep into the Six Rivers National Forest and tucked away in the heart of this forest along that river is a small mountain town by the name of Willow Creek. If you take a stroll down its main street, you'll pass the mechanic, the butcher, the grocery store, the bank, and the sheriff's office. American flags flutter patriotically outside all of the stores and homes.

It would seem at first glance that Willow Creek is no different from any town you may find anywhere across the great United States of America. But Willow Creek is no ordinary town—it's the Sasquatch capital of the world. The Sasquatch is a creature that has existed in the great myths of many cultures for thousands of years. In the Himalayas, he's known as a Yeti. Australians call him a Yowie, and in other parts of the world he goes by Skunk Ape or "oily man" monster. Americans call him a Sasquatch or Bigfoot and he's said to be a towering hairy human-like being that roams the dense old-growth forests of our earth.

What places Willow Creek on the map is the multitude of strange sightings and tales of the Sasquatch that have occurred over the town's recorded history. Many a Willow Creeker will tell you about the bizarre sights they've seen or the blood tingling sounds they've heard. Is there truth to the tales or is this some brilliant marketing ploy carried through the ages? Many in the town believe, some don't care. Most are just grateful for the trickle of tourists eager to go on a Sasquatch hunt or collect one of the many souvenirs for sale. Whatever tickles your fancy: a Sasquatch adorned poster, t-shirt, bottle of wine, mugs, stickers, even a throw rug perhaps? It's hard to make a living in these parts. There are droughts that can choke a farmer's existence; pine bark beetles that can strip a forest bare, leaving it even more susceptible to wildfires; and the big cities that call away the young people for a faster and, debatably, better life.

There are many Willow Creekers who have no time for tall stories or fairy tales, especially one certain inhabitant—Bill Jackson.

If you travel farther west through the town right to the outskirts, you'll come to an almost hidden driveway with an old wood sign, barely hanging on, that notifies you that you've arrived at Jackson Farm. This has been the home of the Jackson family for more than three generations. William Jackson, also known as Bill or Pa, was the son of William. who was the son of William. and there were probably a few Williams before that.

Down the long dirt driveway is the small farm complete with a cozy timber farmhouse and rusty red barn, both could have used a paint job ten years ago. The farm is insulated from the world by trees all around and backs right onto the expansive national forest. There's a scattering of orchard trees, a small paddock of pumpkins that is always ready for Halloween, and then another small paddock for whatever produce he cares for that particular season. It's an honest living, but a hard living; he can manage the farm by himself with a bit of help from seasonal workers and he likes it that way. His wife, Eleanor, passed a few years back and he was estranged from his only child, so he had bitterly resolved himself to the lonely life of a widow.

Bill is a Willow Creeker born and bred; he met his beloved at the local high school. They married young, and they raised their daughter on the

farm. He served for his country as a member of Charlie Company, 1st Battalion, 3rd Marines. Other than a couple of tours of Vietnam, this is where he's spent his life. He had no desire to travel—he'd seen the world in all its nightmares and horrors—he wanted nothing but the kind of peace that only the wind that blows through the fir trees on a clear winter day can provide.

Bill was a no-fuss, black and white, down-the-line kind of man, but sometimes in life the lines become fuzzy. Colors seep in and then sometimes... sometimes you're left with no choice. You can't ignore the magic that surrounds you.

The sun was low in the sky on this particular fall afternoon. Bill and his neighbor Ed had decided to get an afternoon of hunting in before their farms ate up the rest of their days in the harvest months ahead. Bill was gruff in look and in nature, a tall, stocky man with a wiry platinum white beard and crown. He had no care to shave as there was nobody to shave for anymore. He moved stealthily through the forest just a few steps behind Ed. Ed was a foot shorter than Bill but strong and lean; he had a clean, close shave, as close to the bone as possible as it had been every day since his daddy had given him his first razor. He was as gruff and as rough as Bill, maybe even more so. He too had lived the life of a soldier, but his wife had left him decades ago and he had never found another love that could have softened the edges.

The air was cool, it passed right through their bones and frosted their breaths as they pressed on through the thick ancient trees. There was silence all around and they carefully placed their weight on the heavy foliage underfoot hoping not to startle any deer that may be nearby. Bill looked down and frowned, slightly puzzled. Small crimson red flowers dotted the path. They were like summer kisses, delicate and oddly placed for this time of year. They walked on, and the flowers grew in density, blooming gloriously around their feet on the forest floor. Stranger still.

The trees on their path parted and before them was a clearing nestled in a tight circle of trees—a small meadow burgeoning with flora of every shade of sunlight with splashes of royal purple.

"What is this?" Bill asked, his eyes soaking in the wonder.

"Bill," barked Ed as he waved him over.

Bill found Ed standing in front of three chickens gently clucking from within an enclosure made of thick bracken vines.

"My chickens," he muttered. He braced his gun with the trigger finger ready, narrowed his eyes as he looked suspiciously over their surroundings.

Bill cocked his head; he was just as confused.

In the thick ahead, the snap of branches underfoot caught their attention and both—with their hearts pounding—raised their guns toward the sound. Insects began to buzz. Birds chirped across the sky. The high alertness pumped adrenaline through their bodies, their senses heightened and their minds were drawn only to that moment.

The branches and brush on the other side of the clearing parted. The men's trigger fingers tensed. Through the brush stepped what they both recognized from the tales of the town. A Sasquatch. A goddamn Sasquatch. They inhaled sharply. Not taking their eyes off it. They took in its coarse fur, with a red-brown sheen that wisped and curled all over. The beast was huge, about four heads taller than both of them, lean but with bulging muscles. It emanated strength. The pure undeniable brute force of nature. They both felt small, tiny even, as it emerged from behind the trees. It stopped in its tracks and looked directly at them—its big, brown, doe-like eyes frozen in terror as its smooth brown skin creased worriedly.

Mountain lions snarled to each other over the forest. Bill couldn't swallow, but holy mother of Mary, he had never seen anything so amazing. He slowly lowered his gun—he sensed it meant no harm—but Ed held fast. The sounds of insects, birds, and other woodland creatures swelled into a deafening roar as if the whole forest could feel the tension. The Sasquatch gave a low, uneasy growl.

BAM! Ed pulled the trigger. A single shot straight through the heart. The beast crumpled on the spot with only a soft whimper and lay motionless on the ground. The woods were silent once more.

"Jesus, Ed," Bill cried in disbelief at his neighbor's recklessness.

"All this time. I thought it was coyotes taking my chickens," Ed growled.

They both walked over and looked down at the body.

The cold hard skeptic part of their minds took over even though they were staring at the cold hard facts.

"So, what is it?" ventured Bill. "Some kind of mangy bear?"

"I ain't seen no bear that can build a chicken coop," Ed shot back.

Both men stood staring at the body in silence. "Maybe it's… a government experiment?" Bill suggested unconvincingly.

"Designed to steal chickens?" Ed scoffed.

Bill shrugged.

"Ted Jeffries says he's seen Sasquatches in these woods," continued Ed.

"I'm surprised he can see anything after all that moonshine," Bill said dryly.

Both men chuckled uneasily.

Ed sighed, "You've heard the stories. You know where we live."

Bill was about to reply, but a small cry coming from the body of the creature halted their conversation. Ed raised his gun to finish the job.

"Wait," Bill barked. He carefully bent down over the creature and, with great difficulty, rolled up its back. Nestled underneath was a crying baby Sasquatch, still clinging to its dead mama. Bill stopped breathing again, the little creature looked up at him with dewy brown eyes large and round, and full of humanity. His heart melted ever so slightly.

Ed pointed his gun directly at the baby. "Stand back."

Bill calmly raised his arm and placed his hand on Ed's barrel, slowly lowering it.

"Don't," he said firmly.

Ed kept his finger on the trigger. "It's as good as dead out here on its own."

Bill frowned and his heart just ached for this creature, in a way he'd not known his heart to feel for some time. "It's not right. It's just a child."

Ed's laugh echoed across the forest. He raised his gun.

Bill shook his head. "I'll look after it," he said quietly.

Ed lowered his gun again, clearly frustrated. "I know you've been in a bad way since Eleanor, but this thing… it ain't gonna fill her place."

Bill's neck muscles tensed as his crystal blue eyes flicked with a momentary rage of pain. He couldn't just kill this baby or abandon it. There was something inside of him that would not let him be that cold.

The creature was visibly shaking as it began to howl softly. Bill dropped his gun and cautiously picked up the baby—who was at least as big as a toddler—it had the same red-brown fur as his mother with the matching wisps of curls all over.

"Looks like it's a boy," Bill noted as the little orphan continued to cry.

Ed watched both of them with a growing look of disgust.

"You've got enough trouble with your farm and the drought. The economy's bust… don't be wasting your time with some godless Sasquatch," he sneered. "It'll turn on you someday."

The baby wrapped its arms around Bill's neck. It had a deep smell, like an armpit of the earth but Bill felt oddly fine with it.

Ed frowned deeper. "We could make some serious cash from this. Turn our farms around."

Bill shook his head firmly. "And have tourists in our face every day? Journalists? Scientists? The damn government could seize our farms. Are you kidding me? Don't breathe a word of it. To anybody."

Ed nodded reluctantly. He and Bill didn't agree on a lot in life, but they could agree that they wanted nothing to do with anyone from the outside world.

Ed sighed and looked up at the sky. It was going to be dark soon and he wanted to get home. He swung his rifle onto his back and pulled the vines apart on the makeshift chicken coop. He scooped a chicken under each arm and the third he carried in his hands. The chickens clucked and wriggled a little, but mostly obliged. He started to walk away but stopped and turned to face Bill.

"If that thing comes anywhere near my chickens, it's finished," he said with a deep serious tone.

Bill nodded wearily. "He won't. I'll keep him on the farm till he's big enough to fend for himself. Once he's back in the wild, he's on his own."

Bill started to stuff the furry orphan into his coat, trying to replicate the warmth that had drained from his dead mother on the forest floor. "I've gotta get him home and fed, or he won't make it through the night."

"I bet you do, mommy." Ed laughed as he turned and disappeared out of the clearing. He popped his head back through the branches. "I'll keep your secret, Bill. On one condition. You name your new pet Dog," he said, smiling proudly at his own twisted sense of humor.

Bill just nodded absentmindedly as he looked down at the dead mother.

"What about her body?" Bill asked.

"Just leave it for the coyotes," Ed called back as the sound of his footsteps slowly disappeared into the forest.

Bill looked down at the fuzzy little Sasquatch now snuggled into his chest. The creature raised his face, still whimpering, and Bill looked into those big brown eyes. He wondered what he was getting himself into. The scratching of branches caught his attention and he turned his head back toward the dead mother. He took an uneasy step back as long, thick, woody vines sprouted from the earth and wrapped themselves around the lifeless mother's body. He had a mind to call after Ed, but what was the use? He stood watching not knowing what this phenomenon was, but he was transfixed. The vines grew thicker, covering the Sasquatch, then began to pull her body down into the dirt under the forest floor. In a blink, she was gone. Buried. All that remained was a soft mound of earth.

Hairs stood on the back of Bill's neck. Yellow, red, and orange flowers like morning sun breaking the night burst into bloom where the mother once laid. Bill had never before doubted his eyes. Now he questioned every sensible fiber of his being. He'd seen beauty before, but he'd now crossed into a threshold of wonderment he never knew existed. He had stumbled into another world that lay hidden within our own that only a handful are honored to ever see and experience, and now he was beholden to it.

A coyote howled in the distance. Bill bundled the Sasquatch infant deeper in his coat, slung his gun over his shoulder, and took one last look at the clearing. The flowers fluttered gently in the evening breeze and carried the sweetest scent through the forest. Later in life, Bill would often talk of that chilly fall afternoon. He knew that he had lived a life that was full of mistakes, full of misdeeds, and full of regrets, but he had no idea that by giving that creature a second chance, that creature would one day give him his.

The baby's whimper grew louder, so Bill hastily began to trek his way back to the farm. His mind racing, not understanding what he had just seen and how he was going to raise an orphan Sasquatch, but the words of his late father William Senior rang clear. *One step at a time, boy. One step at a time.*

CHAPTER 2
Houseguest

Bill made it back to Jackson Farm just as the last glow of the sun was disappearing behind the surrounding mountains and a chilly mist had taken its hold of the land. While the little Sasquatch snuggled into Bill's chest, he squirmed relentlessly. The child was whimpering, hungry, tired, and aching for that comforting scent and reassuring presence that only a mother can provide.

The old man raced to the farmhouse and stormed across the back porch into the kitchen, a feeling of panic rising in his chest. It had been a while since he had to look after a baby, but he had taken on the responsibility. He rummaged through the fridge and pulled out a tall, thin jar of olives and a carton of milk. Bill moved to the sink and, in his haste, slammed the jar and carton on the countertop. The baby cried louder—scared and confused by all the unfamiliar smells and sounds. Bill patted him and tried to soothe him. "Shhh... shhh," he said with his gravelly voice as he spun off the lid from the jar and splashed the remaining few olives into the sink. After a quick rinse of the jar, he poured in the milk.

Bill swung the cupboard doors open, crouched down to rummage under the sink, and pulled out a kitchen glove. From another drawer, he retrieved some rubber bands and a pair of scissors. He pulled the glove down over the jar and tied it off with the rubber bands, then snipped a tiny hole at the end of the middle finger.

Bill pulled out a chair and sat down. He unzipped his jacket and the little Sasquatch's head popped out, still crying. Bill placed the makeshift bottle into the Sasquatch's mouth, and he immediately clutched it with both his chubby, hairy hands and began to drink. The crying was now replaced with a quiet suckling sound. Bill breathed a sigh of relief, but it was short-lived. The baby drained the milk almost instantly and started to cry again.

"More hey?" said Bill. "Okay, okay," he chuckled, as he filled the jar up again. Bill looked into the Sasquatch's eyes as he drank contentedly. They were deep brown with flecks of gold and huge compared to the size of his plump head, as were his pointy woodland-creature ears. His skin was a smooth leathery walnut-brown, and he had light, fluffy, human-like eyebrows, the same color as his fur. As he suckled the bottle, a little snaggletooth popped over the bottom of his full pinky-brown lips. Bill's heart could not help but melt.

By the end of the feeding session, the infant had finished the entire gallon of milk plus a jar of applesauce. The baby Sasquatch finally stopped crying and snuggled back into the warmth of Bill's chest, but not before letting out a giant burp.

Bill grabbed a few blankets from the linen cupboard and walked down the hallway to the spare room carrying his new companion. The small room was once his daughter's then his granddaughter's, now it would be this little guy's room. With his free hand, he reached for a large, broad cane laundry basket on the bed and tipped out the unfolded clothing. He placed the basket on the floor and lined it with one of the blankets inside, then gently placed the Sasquatch within the basket. He then covered him with the second blanket tucking him in tight, ensuring he was snug and warm.

Bill drew the curtains across the single small window then slumped down next to him, propped up by the wall. In the darkened room lit only by a soft light coming in from under the door, he gently patted the creature. "There, there... Dog," Bill whispered with a voice as soft as crunching gravel. He didn't care much for the name, but he knew it would have to stick if he wanted to appease Ed. Ed was stubborn like that. The Sasquatch rolled his head to look at Bill as he lay there drowsily.

"It's just you and me now, boy… you and your… Pa," Bill said almost fearfully as they looked into each other's eyes. He felt ridiculous saying it, but it was true, he was now this little creature's father.

Bill's thoughts became lost in the memory of the name, Pa. He'd heard it so many times upon the sweet mouths of his daughter and grandchild in this very room. But those same memories were also accompanied by flashes of rage that he quickly had to put them away. Disappointment and bitterness are not what he needed to focus on now.

With a full belly and the most exhausting and emotional day of his young life behind him, the young orphan finally fell asleep. Bill crept out and closed the bedroom door behind him. He lingered a moment and placed his ear against the door to make sure he hadn't disturbed the baby at all. Silence, golden silence. Bill took a moment to catch his thoughts and breath. He shook his head. He had seen a lot of crazy, but this definitely took the prize. The fatigue from the day had overwhelmed him also. He mustered as much willpower as he could and dragged himself back to the kitchen so he too could eat and then slumber.

The night that followed was restless for both the new and old residents of Jackson Farm. Bill could hear the little Sasquatch wailing and howling from the room. He tossed and turned, wanting to comfort him, but he knew that life was tough and without its mother that baby was going to have to learn to fend for himself.

Just before sunrise Bill put on his farm clothes, grabbed himself a coffee, and headed to the Sasquatch's bedroom. As he took some sips of his toasty brew, he frowned with concern—it had been pretty quiet in the room for a while, and he wondered what was going on in there. He opened the door and stood mouth agape.

Dog was sitting up in his basket, clutching a blanket, and sucking his thumb. He looked at Bill placidly. Luscious grass dotted with an array of bright flowers had sprouted through the cracks of the hardwood floorboards from the earth below and surrounded the basket. "What on earth?" Bill exclaimed.

Since Eleanor had passed, each day had been almost like a mirror of the day before. In many ways that is what Bill had held onto for comfort. But now he had a feeling that his new houseguest was about to bring a whole lot of change. Perhaps not the kind of change that Bill wanted, but the kind that was most certainly needed.

Seedling

CHAPTER 3
Growing Pains

Bill Jackson found raising a Sasquatch was some sort of bizarre cross between raising a child, a pet, and an alien—only two of which he had previous experience in. A good dose of discipline, a whole lot of patience, and the oft reliance on good luck was necessary. He had raised a daughter, granddaughter, and a few animals on his farm so he wasn't a complete novice, but there was no handbook for this and, like any parenting experience, some days fared better than others.

Dog was stronger, more agile, and matured faster than a human child. In fact he was up and running within a few weeks of being on the farm. Bill likened it to how a cat or dog raced ahead with their physical development. But Dog was nothing like a dog at all. The old man quickly came to realize that Dog was as intelligent and as sensitive as any human, perhaps even more than some. He had seen a news report on baby sign language and recalled that gorillas had been taught to sign, so he thought he would give it a try. Soon he marveled at Dog's ability to adapt to the language. Bill taught Dog to touch his chin when he was hungry or to hold his hand in a cup and pretend to drink if he was thirsty, and Dog also grunted or pointed to show what he wanted or needed.

Dog was also sensitive to any harshness in the tone of his voice. On the occasions that the old man had to rouse at the infant Sasquatch—to stop him from putting his fingers near the tractor's tiller or stop him eating the produce designated for market—Dog would whimper softly and only be consoled with a little pat and some gentle words. Bill soon understood that Dog responded to the feeling of the words as much as the words themselves.

Like any toddler, Dog's curiosity knew no bounds, each and every thing he encountered was an adventure to be explored. He sniffed, poked, prodded, and touched, and he often broke or licked then tried to eat most everything. Bill was forever pulling shoes, tools, and all sorts of unsavory, inedible, and indigestible objects from his mouth. But after a number of belly aches, Dog did eventually grasp that food was the only thing a little Sasquatch should eat.

Through Dog's infancy, Bill would have seasonal workers help during harvest time. For Dog's safety, he would lock him away in the farmhouse—the television substituted as a perfect babysitter. Bill would sit him on the lounge, in front of the TV with a full loaf of bread smothered with peanut butter and jelly. That kept him out of sight and out of trouble for a good part of the day. It was during those times that Dog developed a keen obsession with National Geographic documentaries and Latin telenovela dramas.

Toilet training was another milestone they had to hurdle. It took Bill a year or so to properly toilet train Dog as his natural instinct was to go wherever he wanted, so in the interim Bill put him in diapers. Dog outgrew the largest kids size pretty quickly, so he had to purchase adult diapers. Bill always felt a little self-conscious when buying them from the young girl at the pharmacy in town. He could have sworn that she always gave him a sort of pity smile. Bill would avert eye contact and get out of there as fast as he could.

Dog loved all things glittery and shiny and would often stop whatever he was doing if something caught his eye—a sparkly stone, a spider web, or water droplet shimmering in the sunlight. Bill would watch as Dog crouched for a closer look as he grinned with admiration at these treasures he found. Bill was always touched by how Dog found such joy in the smallest things in the world that others might take for granted or not even see. In turn it helped Bill to look at the world with fresh eyes.

When it was just the two of them on the farm, Dog liked to follow Bill everywhere; he watched his every move and every word. Dog also liked nothing more than to mimic his guardian's actions, shoveling, hammering nails, even stealing Bill's overalls and wearing them himself. Bill knew it would be some time before Dog would be big enough to return to the wild and so, because of his keen interest in all things farming, he put him to work. Dog's help was so useful that by the time he had grown to an oversized toddler, Bill had halved the amount of outside help he needed to hire for the farm, though he still kept Dog hidden away when any strangers were around.

The most spectacular part of Dog's contribution to the farm was, of course, his gift with nature. Bill soon realized that Dog's connection with nature extended beyond summer flowers to farm produce. When Dog laid his palm on a young seedling, it would grow faster, larger, and be bursting full of its natural flavor. Bill had never known fruit or vegetables that were tastier. Every piece reminded him of being a child and taking that first bite of fruit in the summer or hearty stew that warmed your belly in winter. With Dog's help, each harvest was lush and burgeoning despite the uncertainties that the seasons can bring to a farm.

What struck Bill the most was how easily Dog adapted to his new life on the farm and all things human. He knew there was no way that this creature was simply just an animal—he was human-like for sure, yet he was so much more. Dog was able to understand and comprehend the everyday world around him, but he was inextricably linked to the natural world. Birds and small critters gravitated toward him unafraid. He was so connected to nature that it flowed through him unbounded. Bill could see Dog taste it on the wind, smell and feel it in every blade of grass and bird that called. Bill often wondered if he should let the world know about this discovery, but he knew that greed and power motivated too many. He shuddered to think what would become of his charge if that world ever found him.

With this in mind, Bill tried to teach Dog about the dangers in life; like heat burns, ice can burn too, heights, choking hazards, and how sharp objects cut. The most important lesson, however, was making sure that Dog stayed away from the woods, that he stayed away from humans, and that he stayed away from the world beyond the farm. It was hard for a curious young Sasquatch whose primal instinct was to be with nature to fully understand.

There was one fall morning when Dog had been on the farm for almost a year and was still in diapers but was the size of a five-year-old. He was standing before a pile of boxes containing apples. He placed his hands on the apples and in a matter of seconds, they went from an unripe green, to a full, deep, delicious red.

Bill gave Dog a little pat on the head and Dog smiled as he worked his magic on the final box. "We don't have a lot, but we've got the best. Business is gonna pick up, boy," Bill said proudly.

Dog nodded his head and snorted. Bill turned and loaded those boxes of apples onto the truck and flipped up the tailgate. "I'm heading out, time to get in the barn," he said to Dog over his shoulder as he locked it shut.

He turned around, but there was no Dog. He walked around the truck, "Dog?" he called. Dog was nowhere to be seen, his stomach dropped as he looked out to the back gate of the farm and spotted him running through it toward the woods.

"Ah shoot!" He muttered angrily and started to race after Dog, calling out at the top of his voice, "Dog! No woods!"

Dog looked back but continued to run. "You better stop or else…" Bill hollered.

Dog reached the woods and stopped at the edge as Bill eventually caught up to him. Dog looked up at him with guilty eyes. Bill was out of breath and seething he pointed back to the farm, "Home," he said through clenched teeth. Dog meekly shuffled back.

When they arrived back at the farmyard, Bill ordered Dog into the barn and promptly chained him to a thick column that supported the roof of the barn. Dog started to cry as he desperately tried to pull himself free of the metal cuff from around his foot.

Bill's face dropped in concern. He knew how sensitive Dog was, but he also knew that he had to learn this lesson, "I've told you, you need to stay on the farm where it's safe. They will shoot you. They will hurt you." Dog howled miserably in response.

"You can spend the rest of the day in the barn," Bill said quietly as he turned to leave.

"Pa," came a small voice. It was deep and full, slow and labored but the articulation was undeniable and the word was filled with sadness and sorrow.

Bill stopped at the barn door and spun around to face Dog. "Did. You. Just…?" Bill stopped.

Dog looked up at him with his large, brown, watery eyes. Bill stared back in wonder, this creature continued to amaze him more and more every day. He wanted to rush to him, hug him, celebrate this huge moment, but he knew that there was a more important lesson at play here. He regained his composure, his face hardened.

"Then, you understand. No woods, Dog. No woods." His voice softened a little, "I'll let you out when I get home. I just want you to be safe." Bill hurriedly walked out of the barn before he had a change of heart and locked the doors behind him.

Dog ran to the doors but his chain yanked him back. "Paaa!" he cried.

Outside, he heard the truck door slam and Bill driving away. Dog wiped the tears from his face and dragging his chain, moped over to shelves haphazardly stacked with boxes and crates. He snooped through the Christmas decorations, tools, cords, and odds and ends that Bill couldn't bear to throw out. Finding nothing of interest, he slumped down onto his belly on the earth floor and aimlessly traced his finger in the dirt, leaving a path of grass sprouting behind.

The young Sasquatch sighed and rolled over onto his back where he noticed a large metal wind chime that hung from a shelf. He reached up and gently batted the low hanging tubes. Dusty and covered in webs, the chimes still played a perfect, yet random tune that rang as they caught the morning sun and reflected the light onto the barn walls. Dog pushed the air through his teeth and tightened his lips. "Sh-i-ny," he said to himself as his tongue helped form the words. He reached out and gave the chimes another gentle push, then put his hands behind his head and laid back with a smile.

After that day, Dog never ventured anywhere near the woods, he would sometimes look and wonder what was out there, but the fear of disappointing Pa and of what lay beyond the boundary of Jackson Farm made him never want to find out.

Growing pains aside, the only real blight in those early years was their neighbor Ed. Bill didn't really have any visitors; he had fallen out with his daughter a number of years ago, and, after Eleanor died, other people just dropped off the radar. It was nice to have Ed's company at times. Both were Vietnam Vets, so there was a comradeship they could not find

with most. Ed and Dog, however, seemed to have developed a growing dislike for each other, mostly in part to Ed's undisguised hostility toward Dog. Bill couldn't understand it, but Ed seemed to take great affront to how Bill had bonded with Dog. For Ed's part, he understood people's attachment to animals, but the way that his neighbor fawned over this animal, treating it like his baby—was ridiculous to him. He thought he was worse than one of those Beverley Hills types with their pampered pooches that he'd seen on reality television. Ed was unimpressed with anything about Dog, even when Bill tried to convince him that Dog had sentience way above any other animal. He would have none of it and treated him like an annoying pest.

Bill had made a decision to not tell Ed about Dog's special gifts with nature. He made up all sorts of reasons, but ultimately deep down he knew that he wasn't sure if he could trust Ed. Or anyone for that matter. God was never a word or concept Bill had felt comfortable with, but he believed that Dog had gifts that could only come farm God himself. He had seen what God people had done in this world and what people did to people who were of God. He was going to protect Dog no matter what. Bill saw himself as Dog's custodian, his protector, his Pa. When he was in the army, he had pledged to defend his country. Now he needed to hold the line for something perhaps far more important.

Bill kept the peace with Ed even when he was mean toward Dog just to ensure he remained on side. Ed would often drop by unannounced either by foot or by car as he had on this balmy summer evening when the sun was setting late over the trees. The merry song of the lazuli bunting rang across the fields. Bill and Ed sat on the steps of the back porch, drinking ice cold beer. Dog wrestled with a large rubber ball on the ground in front of them. The ball appeared to be winning.

"So, thought you were gonna release him to the wild," Ed commented snarkily.

"He just…" Bill shrugged, how could he explain that he just knew Dog wasn't ready yet.

Ed waved his hand at Bill not even waiting for an explanation. He knew Bill was attached to this stupid animal, and it was no use. He spied a good number of boxes ready for market on the truck and felt a pang of jealousy at the thought of his barely satisfactory harvest this year. He nodded his head in that direction. "Geez, you've been filling some good produce orders. The rain has helped but… what's your secret? Sasquatch manure?"

Bill kept his eyes straight looking at Dog, "Yeah, that's the secret," he said quietly. He really hated lying. Ed looked at him puzzled but was distracted by Dog who tumbled over from trying to wrestle the ball.

Ed shook his head. "Gosh, he's stupid, ain't he?" he scoffed.

Bill's eyes flinched. "He's just a toddler, Ed."

Ed looked at Bill incredulously. "What… all of a sudden, you're the Bigfoot whisperer?

Bill remained eyes front. "I know a thing or two," he said calmly as he took a swig of his beer.

Dog's ball bounced away from him and landed at Ed's feet. He scooped it as Dog ran over to him to retrieve it. Ed held it up high, out of reach. Dog jumped for it. Ed then teased him by lowering it and raising it high again as Dog lurched.

"I heard you could speak," he said to Dog, his eyes narrowing. "If you ask nicely, I'll give it back."

Dog continued to jump and swipe for the ball in Ed's hand. "Come on. Let's hear it," Ed taunted.

Dog paused for a minute. He looked at Ed and gave a low short growl then walked away. Ed took aim with a malicious grin and pegged the ball at Dog's head. Dog yelped, but happily chased the ball as it bounced away.

Bill looked at Ed disapprovingly.

Ed shrugged. "Where I come from, an animal knows its place."

He nodded a goodbye at Bill, who watched him as he walked to his truck and drove off. Bill was not impressed; he knew there was so much this little Sasquatch needed to learn.

"Get over here, boy," he called to Dog.

Dog scurried over with his ball. Bill got down to Dog's level and looked him straight in the eyes. Dog stared back with eyes as open as his heart.

"Dog, you've got a voice. If you want things in life, you're going to need to use it," Bill said with a low serious voice.

Dog paused and frowned then held up the ball and smiled. "Ball!" he exclaimed as he threw the ball, and he chased after it again.

Bill smiled proudly, but his face gradually clouded over as he watched Dog roll and tumble in a tussle with his round foe. He was so innocent and sweet, and Bill knew he wasn't going to be able to keep him safe forever.

The frustrations with their neighbor aside, the days on Jackson Farm were idyllic in many ways for the farmer and the Sasquatch. They worked together, they ate together, and, in fact, they did most things together. As time passed, Bill grew attached to his little companion. He found himself enjoying his company, relishing his milestones, and celebrating his achievements.

The favorite part of both of their day was their shared meals together, especially dinner. As they sat at the dining table, Bill would regale Dog with stories of his childhood on the farm and his life with Eleanor, but Dog was particularly interested in his experiences in the jungles of Vietnam. As Bill told him about the friends that never came back, Dog would thumb through Bill's military books, horrified yet fascinated by the images of destruction and death. For a young Sasquatch who cherished life, he was saddened by the pain that humans caused each other. Bill tried to teach Dog about anger and rage and impress upon him how violence is sometimes necessary, but it never really solves the true issues. Dog would listen attentively even though Bill wasn't really sure if he understood. Regardless, there was a certain comfort in the exchange for both of them.

One evening when Dog was slightly older and finally out of diapers, they had finished a meal and were sitting at the table enjoying each other's company. Dog had been staring thoughtfully at a picture of Eleanor on the side table. Dog pointed at the picture and then at himself and grunted. He did it a few times with urgency.

"Eleanor? My wife?" Bill asked, confused.

Dog grunted and pointed at the picture again and then at himself. "Mmm… om', he slowly got out.

He had been experimenting with new words and was picking them up by the day.

"Mom? Your Mom?" Bill frowned as his heart sank. Dog nodded urgently.

"You want to know about your mother," Bill nodded sadly. He had wanted to avoid this conversation since the day it happened. He knew the truth was ugly and too painful.

"I found you in the woods, just a little baby. I…" Bill's voice trailed off as he looked down at the table, his guilt rendered him voiceless. Even though it wasn't by his hand she had fallen, he had always wondered whether he could have done more? Should he have done more?

Dog gave a little moan. He knew something terrible had happened to her. He had seen enough National Geographic documentaries to understand what went on in the wild. He shuddered. With his head hanging low, without a word, Dog got up out of his chair and left the room.

"Goodnight, Dog," Bill said quietly after him, unsure what to do or what to say to console him.

Dog walked into his darkened room and slumped on the bed. He had seen mothers on the television shows he had watched. They always hugged and loved and protected their children no matter what. He couldn't imagine she would ever leave him. Something had happened. He had an ache, it was like loneliness but was deeper and wider and had been there since he could remember. Even though Bill was always just down the hallway, this feeling was heaviest in the solitude and silence of night. It was a feeling that he'd never had a word for. Now he knew that word was *mom*.

CHAPTER 4
All Things Shiny

As the days turned into years, Dog became more and more human. Bill knew the wild was no place for him, and he feared it never would be. He wanted to be just like his Pa, and his Pa indulged him in his quirks even when that little voice at the back of his mind told him this may not be the best for a beast that needs to return to the wild someday. All they could do was press on with the life they had. So they continued to work together to build Jackson Farm into an in-demand produce supplier.

Dog had grown almost as tall as Bill—the top of his head now reached Bill's nose—though he was far stockier with arms and legs of bulking strength. Dog's face was also maturing now that the chubbiness had dropped off and his eyebrows had thickened. His formerly pudgy fingers were long and lean, with thick nails the color of his skin. He was like a big kid—just way bigger.

Life on Jackson Farm had a pretty consistent rhythm. Each morning at sunrise, rain, hail, shine, or snow, Bill would be dressed in his work overalls and preparing his morning coffee. He would give a short, sharp whistle, and Dog would burst out of his room also dressed in his denim overalls. Bill now had to buy Dog a larger size than his own as Dog kept splitting the seams on the ones he'd been borrowing from him.

After a hearty breakfast, which usually consisted of multiple eggs, slices of bread, and bowls of fruit, they would head out the back door. Bill would put on his Outback leather hat, and they would both put on their work boots. Despite the fact that his tough feet didn't require shoes, Dog had begged Bill to buy them. Sometimes Bill joked that if Dog looked in the mirror, he would be shocked to see a Sasquatch staring back at him. He couldn't understand why Dog insisted on having shoes, but he appreciated that Dog liked to do things that humans do and once again indulged him.

Dog was always ready and raring for a day of farming; he relished the hard work and the company. Such was Dog's contribution, now that he was bigger, they didn't need additional outside help at all. It was just the two of them, and that's how they liked it. He would excitedly run up to Bill and help him push the wheelbarrow or carry the shovel, rake, and hoe and then race off toward the fields.

The two would spend endless hours in the fields. Dog loved to grow things, so he would kneel in a large patch of earth, carefully planting seeds one-by-one. He would gently push a seed into the dirt, lovingly cover it with soil, then water it with a watering can. He would then cup his hands over the small mound and feel the flow of the world pass through him into that tiny seed. Each time, he would smile broadly as his seed sprouted moments later.

Every mid-morning they would stop for a break. Dog liked to head over to his favorite tree stump in the middle of the fields and have his snack alone there. He would sit and eat, and the birds would perch on his shoulder as he fed them crumbs from whatever was on the menu, which was normally peanut butter and jelly sandwiches. The stump had once been a magnificent solitary tree where an infant Dog had sat finding relief under its shady branches.

After a particularly long spell of drought a year or so back, the tree had withered and had been overrun by some sort of tree-eating bug. Dog had spent many days laying his hands on that tree trying to heal it, but even he could not bring it back from the brink. Bill had grimly handed him an axe and, even though Dog whined, he knew what had to be done. It was a reminder to both of them that nothing could escape the final end—special Sasquatch powers or not.

After the mid-morning break, they would resume their chores and by the end of each working day Dog had transformed his patch of dirt into a rich, green fledgling crop, or an already green field into rows and rows of vital fruit and vegetables. For Dog, the favorite part of his day was the reward for his work, which usually involved some large volume of food and a television show or two.

On one particular midsummer afternoon, Bill and Dog—both dusty and sweaty from their working morning—stood side by side and surveyed the day's work. Bill gave Dog a huge pat on his back. "Nice job, boy."

Dog beamed with pride as they looked over the baby zucchini sprouts peeking out and greeting the world.

"Go clean up, then you can watch your show," Bill said.

Dog chortled with excitement and bolted off toward the farmhouse. Bill shook his head laughing and smiling to himself as he followed behind much slower.

A few moments later, Dog sat upright on the couch, riveted to the TV. On-screen was his favorite show—*Los Pecados De Los Santos*, which translates to The Sins of the Saints. A sweeping, melodramatic saga about a beyond your wildest dreams wealthy dynasty and their loves, losses, and intrigues.

A beautiful young couple stood facing each other. The flawlessly gorgeous woman with flowing ebony locks spoke, "Angelo, I love you. I don't care that your child is my aunty, or that you framed me for your murder."

The camera focused on a dark-haired man with glorious muscles bulging from beneath his preppy polo shirt. He pulled the woman close. "Shhh, my sweet, no talk of the past," he whispered softly as he kissed her passionately. He broke from her lips, overcome with emotion. "Marry me, Sofia. Let me make this right," he exclaimed as the dramatic music crescendoed.

The screen door in the kitchen slammed and Dog's face flicked with annoyance, he didn't like having his TV viewing disturbed. Bill entered the room carrying the day's mail and dumped it on the coffee table in front of Dog.

"Your brain is gonna turn to mush," Bill teased as he joined him on the couch.

Dog ignored him as Bill also became absorbed in *Los Pecados De Los Santos*.

Sofia began to weep. Angelo held her face in his hands, bewildered. "I hope these are tears of joy?" he asks.

Bill wasn't following, he nudged Dog with his elbow. "Did she say yes?"

Dog waved at Bill and grunted, not wanting to miss the action. Sofia pushed Angelo away and sashayed over to the window and looked out forlornly then swung back around flicking her hair perfectly as tears filled her eyes. "Oh, Angelo, how do I tell you this?" she wailed.

Angelo was even more confused, "Tell me what baby?"

"I'm pregnant," Sofia says as she shook her mane and pouted. The camera zoomed in and held onto her face for dramatic effect then crossed to Angelo who was bursting with joy.

"That's wonderful news," he exclaimed as he rushed to Sofia to hold her.

Sofia shook her head and threw herself on his bulging chest.

"No… it's Father Santiago's."

The camera zoomed onto Angelo's face as it dropped in shock and held it there for many uncomfortable moments as the music climaxed and credits began to roll.

Dog threw his head back and groaned in disappointment.

"You're a sucker for romance," Bill chuckled as he turned off the TV with the remote.

Dog noticed the mail and picked up an envelope. He sniffed it and had a chew of the corners before his eye caught a picture of a trophy on the cover of a magazine in the pile. He snatched it up and stared intently. The cover read "14th Annual Trinity County Fair." Dog smiled dreamily and said, "Shiny." It was the prettiest shiny thing he had ever seen. All golden and polished.

"You do like your shiny things." Bill smiled. "That's a trophy, it's yours if you can grow the biggest pumpkin at the fair." Dog's eyes opened wide as he jumped up and ran with the magazine into the kitchen.

He hurriedly swung open the pantry doors and saw a pumpkin on the shelf. He grabbed it and put it down on the kitchen table next to the magazine. Bill followed him into the kitchen and stood at the doorway watching.

Dog placed his leathery hands on the pumpkin and concentrated. After a moment, the pumpkin began to grow, the flesh expanding along with the skin. Dog looked over to Bill and grinned so wide his snaggletooth popped out. Bill nodded in encouragement.

Dog returned his focus to the pumpkin. He closed his eyes and the pumpkin continued to grow at a rapid pace, when suddenly… POP. The pumpkin exploded all over Dog's face and the kitchen. Bill laughed loudly as he wiped pumpkin bits and pieces from his own face.

"You're not gonna grow one of those gigantic pumpkins overnight. It's gonna take time to get it right. You've gotta get the right seeds, gotta look after it, and, sure, you can use your hands, but you're gonna need a whole lotta mother nature."

Dog stared at the magazine cover and gently licked away the pumpkin seeds and juice he could reach with his tongue. He had learned about how humans collected things from a television show, and so had begun his own shiny collection with rocks and trinkets he had found in the house and around the farm. Dog had never wanted anything more in his life than to add that gleaming trophy to his shiny collection.

CHAPTER 5
Eye on the Prize

Over the next few years Dog held onto his vision, and he soon realized that even with his mastery of nature, growing a giant, healthy pumpkin was a major undertaking. Ultimately, he was at the mercy of the seasons. If the winter frost was particularly early and cold on a given year, or if warmer summer days lasted well into September, the weather would change the hardiness of the vegetable, weaken the shell, and even with the slightest laying of hands he would find himself cleaning up another gourd explosion.

Still, the maturing Sasquatch kept his eye on the prize. Each summer he would plant his seeds, and he would hover like a hen over her brood, tending to and caring for them in between all his other farm duties. Bill encouraged his hobby. He watched as Dog eagerly looked forward to the leaves changing and the chill that would start to tinge the air. Dog knew it was another chance to win his shiny trophy. Bill coached and guided him and they both learned a thing or two about patience, disappointment, and hope. As well as the many perfect ways to bake, steam, fry, or sauté the exploded pumpkins and their seeds.

By the time Dog was a teen Sasquatch, he had grown to be seven feet tall, and his whole body was packed with bulging muscle covered in wispy, wavy fur. His soft leathery, light brown skin was ever so slightly lined from age, while his head had finally caught up to his ears and eyes which were now in perfect proportion. Those gilded-brown eyes still gleamed with a mischievousness, though he was definitely more thoughtful and quiet in his older age. His face was crowned with glorious auburn tendrils whose ends had been sunkissed to rusty gold.

The years had not dampened his prize pumpkin ambitions even with many failures and disasters behind him. This fall, however, was different. The weather gods had been far kinder to his prospects, no early frost or late summer—just a perfect blend of one season to the next.

It was a brisk mid-fall evening, the sun was barely holding onto the sky when Dog and Bill now stood in front of his pumpkin. And my, what a pumpkin it was, an enormous beauty and, this time, the shell was perfect and was holding firm.

Dog looked at Bill with wide, hopeful eyes. "Trophy?"

Bill chuckled, "Maybe. The fair's this weekend, I'd say you've still got some growing to do." Dog nodded enthusiastically.

"We got an early start tomorrow." He gave Dog a pat on the back. "Night, boy," said Bill and walked off to the farmhouse leaving Dog alone with his pumpkin.

Dog gave his big orange baby one last gentle pat and smiled lovingly at it then headed over to the barn where his bedroom now was. His old room in the farmhouse could no longer contain him, and when his bed finally broke under his weight, Bill was worried the old floorboards would be next, so they found a better arrangement.

Dog entered the dark barn and closed the large creaky doors behind him. He walked across the floor and flipped a switch on the wall. The barn was instantly illuminated by gentle, sparkling white fairy lights that were strung across the rafters and over his bed.

Under the window sat his bed with a frame large and sturdy enough to support the growing adolescent Sasquatch. Made out of spare metal lying around the farm, the frame and the mattress were entwined with luscious grass, vines, and flowers sprouting from the dirt floor. Dog often loved to sit on his bed and watch the stars and seasons as they moved across the world just outside his window.

On a small table beside his bed was his shrine, an homage to his love of all things shiny. Upon it he had carefully arranged his collection of sparkly trinkets and treasures that he had accumulated over the years, including a mirror ball Pa had gifted him and a glitter lava lamp that Pa had kindly ordered for him after he saw an infomercial on TV. Sitting in the direct center was a framed picture of the, so far elusive, pumpkin trophy.

Dog moved to another wooden side table near his bed where an old record player sat. A few years back, Dog had found it in one of the many overstuffed storage shelves on the opposite wall and had been immediately transfixed. Pa showed him how to use it and helped him fish out Eleanor's old collection of vinyl records. He had been hooked on music ever since. Especially the music of an old Australian singer called John Farnham that Eleanor had been fond of after a trip to Australia in her youth. Dog understood exactly why because the emotion in his voice gave him chills every time.

He lifted the record player arm and then placed the needle on the spinning record. The rhythmic piano riff of his favorite John Farnham song "One" began to play. Dog smiled. He loved music; he swayed a little, stepped from side to side, and added in a full turn, just like he'd seen in the music videos on TV. He soaked in the music and the words, then shuffled over to the window, displaying a surprisingly good sense of musical timing and rhythm for a towering, bulky, long-limbed Sasquatch.

He stopped at the barn window looking out at the farmhouse just as Bill's bedroom light turned off, and he whimpered sadly. The lyrics of "One," a song about being lonely, rang all too true. For Dog, nighttime still always felt the loneliest.

A breeze gently tinkled the wind chimes that were now hanging outside of his barn window. Dog's hair stood on end, he froze, he sniffed the air, catching a scent on the breeze. He frowned. A strange, yet oddly familiar scent. The chimes quietened as the night wind stopped. Dog sniffed the air again… nothing.

He lingered at the window a moment longer and looked out to the woods. The sky was cloudy with no visible stars or moon, so it all just faded into darkness. He gave a little anxious snort. The song had stopped by now, so he walked over to the turntable and gently lifted the needle and placed it back on the record. He took off his work overalls and hung them over a chair at the end of his bed, then took off his boots and carefully placed them under the same chair. Despite his innate wildness, he liked to keep things neat and tidy.

He climbed into bed and, even though his feet protruded off the end, he felt cozy and snug indeed. He turned his head and looked up at his trophy picture for a long time, thinking pleasing thoughts about holding his shiny prize. He let out a deep sigh and reached for the light switch and flicked it off. Dog rolled over and fell into delightful dreams of tiny little pumpkins dancing through the woods.

CHAPTER 6
A Visitor

The next morning proved to be a glorious fall day, soft sunlight spread over the mountains as the crisp air made Dog's breath feel all that more alive. After the fields were tended to, Dog and Bill had set to work under the bonnet of the truck to give it a tune-up. Bill leaned over beside him, offering direction and pointing at the different parts of the engine.

"Tighten these two, then we're done," he said as Dog happily obliged, then frowned.

"Oil?" he asked.

"Yeah, it's probably due." Bill nodded, impressed.

He paused and looked at the towering creature in front of him hunched under the engine and shook his head in amazement. "I reckon you'd be able to run this farm on your own, Dog," he said.

Dog smiled at Bill as he beamed up at him with pride. Dog's face dropped. He pulled his head out from under the bonnet and looked down the long driveway into the distance.

"Car," he said quietly.

"Good ears. Quick," Bill said as Dog followed their stranger-approaching drill. He hurried into the barn, swiftly pulling the doors closed behind him.

Bill watched with a frown as a small brown hatchback pulled up to the rear of the house, and a young lady stepped out of the vehicle and slowly approached. Her flowing brown hair with blonde tips haloed a sweet, open face. Bill frowned at the young woman as she walked, but when he looked into her large green eyes the realization hit him.

"Jessie?" he asked.

The young lady stood awkwardly in front of Bill. "Pa." She smiled.

Bill smiled with sadness. "Jessica? Lord. I haven't seen you since…" Bill paused, but he knew exactly when. He had stewed on that moment for years since.

"Just before Gran died," Jessie said softly.

Bill nodded solemnly.

They stared at each other, not knowing what to say. "Got your postcards. You've seen a lot of the world," Pa offered.

"Yeah, I wanted to get away," Jessie shrugged.

Bill's face clouded. "Yeah, I'm sure you did."

Jessie's face flinched with a hint of pain, and she took a slow breath. "I hope you don't mind me just dropping in?" she said, unsure of how to deal with this reception.

Bill's coolness melted. "No, no. Not at all. Seven years… Gosh. Come here." He reached out and drew her in for the warmest of hugs. "Come on inside. I can make you a coffee, but I'm not like your Gran. I don't have tons of treats stashed away in the cupboard to stuff you with," he said fondly.

They both smiled at each other as they walked into the farmhouse side by side. Bill looked over his shoulder with a worried glance wondering what was going on in the barn. He hesitantly closed the screen door behind him.

Pretty soon, Jessie and Bill found themselves in the living room sitting opposite each other in silence. After the niceties had been taken care of, what was left to say hung between them in the air. Jessie took an anxious sip from her glass of water and looked around the room. It was just as she remembered it—old mismatched furniture, wooden floorboards, and a stone fireplace. It still gave her a cozy feeling as there were so many memories in this room. There was also a dank old smell, like that of an animal, but she didn't remember Pa ever having a dog. Still, it was neat and well kept.

"How old are you now?" Pa queried, interrupting her train of thought.

"Twenty-two," Jessie replied.

"Married?" he continued.

Jessie looked at him incredulously. "Pa! At twenty-two?"

Bill smiled. "I married your grandmother at eighteen."

Jessie shook her head, also with a smile, as she took another sip from her glass. "Do you have a job?" asked Pa.

"I work part-time at the mall," she shrugged.

"The mall's not a career," he frowned.

"I'm studying to become a nurse," Jessie shot back.

"That's a good job. Helping people." He nodded approvingly, and she smiled in reply. Bill cleared his throat and looked steely at her, "Heard from your father?"

Jessie's head dropped a little as she had yet another drink of water. "Not for a while," she said quietly.

"Probably hatching his latest scam," he spat, unable to contain himself.

Jessie took a deep breath and sat up straight and looked him directly in the eyes, "Pa... Mom has cancer."

Bill inhaled quietly but sharply. They both sat there for many moments.

"How bad?" Bill asked quietly.

"She's going through chemo," she replied.

Bill considered this for a moment. "She know you're here?"

Jessie shook her head and looked at him earnestly. "Given the circumstances, I was hoping you'd come visit her."

Bill felt his chest seize tight with anger, disappointment, and pain. He looked away, "We have nothing left to say. She made her choices a long time ago."

A tear escaped from Jessie's eye, which she quickly wiped away, then she rose to her feet. She had expected this response, even prepared for it, but his stubbornness and coldness still stung.

"I'm going to get some more water," she mumbled as she hastened to the kitchen with her half-full glass in hand.

Bill sat stunned by the news. He had long ago resigned himself to the fact that he would never speak to his daughter again. He had dissected those painful events so many times, far too many times, and he had always come to the same conclusion—unforgivable. The betrayal, the pain she had inflicted on her sick mother, the ease in which she chose that man over everything.

Bill's tirade of thoughts were interrupted by a shriek from Jessie's that filled the house.

He jumped to his feet and raced into the kitchen. Jessie was behind a kitchen chair in one corner of the room, pointing and screaming at Dog who was crouched fearfully in the other corner. Bill stood between them in the middle of the room and raised his palms to Jessie in an attempt to alleviate her fears.

"It's okay. This is Dog," he said calmly. He looked at Dog who shielded his face with his arms. "Dog, meet Jessie."

Jessie was still hysterical. "That's not a dog!" she screamed.

Dog moved his hands to cover his ears.

Bill turned to Jessie. "Well, that's his name," he explained patiently.

Dog grunted and timidly stood to his full height, still with his hands over his ears just in case. This pretty human was particularly loud.

Jessie's eyes widened in terror as she looked up at the huge beast. Her heart pounding wildly. "Keep it away from me," she screamed at Bill.

Bill reached out to touch her arm, as he tried to calm her. "Jessie, it's okay, he's harmless," he said softly.

Dog nodded in agreement from behind him. Jessie was unconvinced and gripped her kitchen chair tighter, ready to brandish it as a weapon. The sliver of calmness in her mind did reason that if Pa was so calm, there must be a reason to not freak out. The adrenaline, however, continued to have control over her body.

"But what is it?" she frowned. Her voice still an octave higher than usual.

Bill tilted his head and looked at her intently. "Jess, you grew up round here, you know what *he* is. He's a Sasquatch."

Jessie's eyes widened, the tales of her childhood rushed back. They had made her sleep under her covers, quiver if there were any noises outside her window in this very house, scared some beast would snatch her away at night. The myth, the marketing, the tourists on their hunts.

"I… don't… I just thought it was a hoax, you know, to make money."

"Me too, but I've had him since he was a baby. Found him orphaned in the woods." Bill turned his head to Dog who, up until that moment, had been standing in fear—fear of this visitor, but more scared because he had broken the rules. He was supposed to never leave his barn when visitors came.

Bill nodded. "Get over here, boy."

Dog timidly stepped behind Bill, even though he towered over him. "Go say hello, Dog," Bill urged.

Jessie looked up at him warily.

"He's not met a woman before," said Bill as he smiled at Jessie.

"In fact, the only other human he's met is our neighbor Ed."

Dog took a step toward Jessie but looked back with uncertainty at Pa.

"Go on," Bill encouraged.

Dog stepped closer to Jessie and leaned in to sniff her hair. Jessie stood deadly still.

"Flowers," Dog said.

Jessie's heart raced. "Oh, God. Oh, God. He talks?" She looked at Bill amazed.

Bill chuckled. "He's full of surprises."

Dog took an interest in Jessie's long hair and began to play with it, watching it gently fall through his fingers like strands of sunshine.

Jessie was nervous, but didn't stop him. "This is absolutely crazy," she whispered.

Bill affectionately looked up at Dog and rubbed his fur then his face clouded with concern. He turned to her. "Jessie, I need you to keep this a secret. If word got out, well, people just wouldn't understand. Lord only knows what those scientists would do to him."

He absentmindedly continued to tousle Dog's hair as he became lost in the fear of that future. Jessie watched Bill's affection toward this beast; she studied Dog's face and saw a sweetness. An innocence in his eyes. She nodded solemnly. "I won't tell anyone, Pa."

Dog by now was confident that Jessie posed no threat. He took her by the hand and started to lead her out the kitchen door. She looked back at Bill, unsure. Bill shrugged with a smile.

"Looks like you made yourself a friend."

"It's massive," Jessie exclaimed as she stood with Dog and Bill looking at Dog's potential prize pumpkin.

Bill nodded. "He's close. Real close."

Dog smiled and clapped. "Trophy!"

Bill smiled and raised a pair of crossed fingers. "Three days before we find out… keep at it."

Dog sighed. Bill cocked his head to the side and motioned it to the fields.

"Right now there's a farm here that's not gonna farm itself."

Dog whimpered as he looked at Jessie. "I'll stay around for a while," she assured him. Satisfied, Dog happily trotted off to the fields.

Not long after, Dog was on his hands and knees in freshly churned earth as Bill and Jessie watched him from several feet away. Jessie shook her head incredulously at Bill, "I can't believe you've turned Dog into a farmer."

"He does the work of four men."

Jessie frowned. "Isn't that kind of exploiting him?"

Bill paused looking at Dog thoughtfully. "I've been conflicted at times, but no," he answered. "The two of us can run this place alone and he can stay safe." He pointed at Dog. "Besides, he loves it."

Jessie watched as Dog cupped a mound of dirt with his hands. A shoot began to grow into a larger plant. Jessie gasped. "Did that just grow… like really fast?"

Bill chuckled. "Yep. Dog is… special."

Jessie turned to Bill with eyes wide in wonderment. "But how's that even possible?"

Bill shrugged his shoulders. "Good green thumb? I've wondered about it since I found him. It's like he's at one with nature. That he's nature himself?"

"He's… he's magic," Jessie whispered. Jessie's wonder was interrupted by an alarm ringing on her phone. She retrieved it from her back pocket and looked at the screen. "Oh no. I've got something to do, I should probably get going."

Bill's face dropped in disappointment. "Okay then."

"Dog! I gotta go now," Jessie called. Dog jumped up and ran to Jessie, grabbing her by the hand.

"Stay. Stay," he begged.

Jessie giggled, "I wish I could, but—"

"Stay!" said Dog sadly.

Bill looked at his granddaughter, he didn't realize how much he had missed this. "Why don't you stay for dinner?"

Dog was excited by the prospect of company. "Dinner!" he exclaimed.

Bill smiled. "He's not going to take no for an answer."

Jessie was smiling too, "Let me make a phone call." Dog jumped up and down with joy. He was so taken with this visitor who smelled like a spring garden and brought so much sunshine to his day that he wanted to keep her here as long as he could.

CHAPTER 7
Good Times

Later that evening, Dog sat at the dining room table while Bill poured wine for himself and Jessie. Jessie was serving spaghetti and meat sauce from a big cooking pot onto plates for Bill and herself. She was about to give Dog his serving, when Bill spoke up.

"Just give him the pot."

Jessie raised an eyebrow. "Seriously?"

Bill nodded so she removed Dog's plate and placed the cooking pot in front of him, then took a seat. Dog was eager to get started. Bill raised his glass of wine. "As they say, when you eat, remember the farmer."

Jessie raised her glass also. "To the farmers."

Dog was uninterested in anything they were saying, he was already using his fingers to scoop up and devour as much spaghetti as possible.

Bill noticed Jessie's look of shock. "He never took to forks."

"Or napkins, it seems," Jessie grimaced at Dog's mess and handed him a paper napkin. Dog was confused by the gesture, surveyed the napkin then promptly gobbled it down with his spaghetti.

"No, Dog!" Jessie exclaimed.

Bill broke into a wide grin. "I've seen him eat worse."

They both roared with laughter, but Dog was oblivious to the fuss and resumed his eating, ignoring any form of decorum or etiquette.

After their plates were empty and their bellies content, Dog, Bill, and Jessie sat around the table talking.

"Did Grandma ever meet Dog?" Jessie asked, as she looked down at the old framed photo she was holding of her grandmother in her twenties. She smiled fondly at her tight curls and full petticoat dress.

Bill's heart dropped a little at the memory, "Nah, I found him not long after she passed. It's been good to have the company."

"BRPPPPPP." Dog interrupted with a huge belch.

"And entertainment," he said dryly as he and Jessie broke into laughter again.

Jessie reached for Dog's shoulder and gave him a gentle push. "Gross, Dog!" Dog beamed as he lapped up the attention. She looked at the photo again and her face clouded with sadness.

"She passed so suddenly," she whispered.

Bill nodded with heaviness, the loss still pained him, "She went to sleep, then never woke up."

Jessie traced the edge of the photo frame with her finger. "Mom really misses Grandma. She mentions her a lot."

The fury and bitterness from those many years ago hit him like a slap. Bill's nose flared as his shoulders squared up. "Is that right? She didn't even go to her mother's funeral."

Jessie was sweet in nature and generally non-confrontational. She really wanted to keep the peace, but knew that all of them carried wounds from that time so long ago. Jessie kept her head down. "I told you, Pa, she didn't want to create a scene. She said goodbye in her own way."

Bill's eyes raged. "She sided with your crooked father. I never saw either of you after that."

Jessie grimaced as the room fell deathly silent. Jessie took a sip of wine, not quite knowing what to say. She understood the way he felt. Her parents, especially her father, had caused such pain. Her grandparents had practically raised her when her parents were going through all sorts of trouble. She understood his anger, she carried her own from that time. She was wise enough to know that if Pa and her mother didn't sort this out now... there may not be another chance.

Bill stared down at the table then he looked at Jessie; he sensed her sadness and felt a little ashamed. He knew this wasn't anything to do with her, she was just a child when all this happened.

He started in a gentle gruffness. "Look, I know you mean well, and it's clear your mom raised you right, it's just…"

Dog who had been observing this all the while and sensed the awkwardness looked back and forth between Bill and Jessie. He broke into a smile. "Snap!" he interrupted.

"What?" said Jessie confused.

Bill smiled. "He wants to play cards."

"Really?" laughed Jessie. Dog ran off to get the cards quite chuffed at the distraction he had caused.

"Yeah, but keep an eye on him, he cheats," said Bill wryly.

The plates were now cleared and a bowl of grapes sat on the table. Dog and Jessie were playing cards while Bill sat back and watched. Jessie reached for some grapes under Dog's watchful gaze. In the brief second her eyes were off the game, Dog moved with sniper precision, seized the opportunity, and laid down a non-matching card.

He immediately slammed the table. "SNAP," he cried.

Jessie eyed him suspiciously, "Wait! Are you sure that was a snap… show me!"

Dog ignored her and picked up the cards and quickly shuffled them, looking rather pleased with himself. Jessie looked to Bill with a shocked face that pleaded for help.

Bill raised his palms in surrender. "I'm not getting involved," he said with a smile.

He poured himself some wine then topped-up Jessie's glass. She didn't take her eyes off the cards as she picked up the glass and sipped.

"Thanks," she said without turning or looking.

Bill chuckled. "I see you've learned your lesson."

He sat back in his chair and took a sip from his glass looking at his granddaughter. He could see Eleanor in her eyes and hair, which was comforting and sad at the same time.

"So, you got a boyfriend? he asked.

Jessie remained focused on the game. "Not at the moment. Mom's been my main priority."

Bill's chest wells with pride, whatever had happened between him and his daughter, Jessie had always been a good kid. He also knew whatever issues he had with his daughter, he had to make sure they were all right.

"That's a lot of responsibility for you," he said in his raspy softness. "Is she being looked after properly? Got good insurance? Are you guys doing okay with money?"

Jessie stopped the game and looked at Bill with eyes of gratitude. "We're fine, but thanks."

BANG! Dog slapped the cards on the table. "SNAP," he said enthusiastically as he scooped up the pile of cards into his possession.

Jessie looked at him through narrow eyes. "Congratulations, Dog." Her voice dripping in disbelief.

Bill laughed from his belly. "He's getting shiftier in his old age."

"How old is he?" she queried looking at his strong body with fur that had a glowing sheen.

"Don't know," Bill shrugged. "He's growing so damn fast. He's been on the farm six years tomorrow, but it's like he's a teenager… about eighteen, maybe?"

"Wait!" Jessie exclaimed. "Tomorrow is like his birthday!" She clapped with excitement, her eyes dancing. "Are you having a party?"

Bill waved her away. "We don't do parties."

"Aww, come on!" Jessie urged. She felt so sorry for Dog cooped up on this farm, even her grandfather could do with a little more fun.

"Party!" Dog chimed in. The word party had piqued Dog's interest, he had seen a lot of parties on his favorite shows and they always involved all sorts of delicious foods and sometimes shiny gifts.

Jessie was getting excited now; she had loved her day on the farm. "Pa, I can drop by tomorrow morning, bring a small cake. Is that okay?"

Bill smiled and threw his hands in the air as a sign of giving in. He hadn't felt so relaxed like this for a very long time.

Jessie clapped her hands excitedly. "Dog, we're having a party!"

Dog also clapped with excitement, he sensed this party would be different from a TV party, but it would still be good all the same, especially since it was his. His own party! He felt his heart burst with happiness. This visitor was like sunshine. However, his mind quickly returned to his main concern, the card game at hand. He grunted at Jessie as he motioned to the cards and frowned determinedly. He hadn't finished winning. Jessie and Bill once again broke into laughter.

The sun was setting and a deep coolness was beginning to settle on the land. Jessie, Bill, and Dog stood around Jessie's car. Despite the chill in the air, they all had the warm glow that comes from an evening of good food, good company, and good times.

Jessie gave Bill a hug. "It's been a wonderful evening." She stepped back as a sad frown formed. "Please think about visiting Mom. Here's her details just in case." She handed him a business card for the hospital. Bill's face didn't move, and he said nothing, but he placed the card in his pocket. Jessie's face also remained emotionless, but deep in her heart she was grateful that he at least took it.

Jessie turned to Dog and wrapped her arms around him and squeezed him tight. "It was very nice to meet you, Dog," she said as she snuggled into his fur. Dog soaked in the affection; he was having one of the best days of his life. He wished he could have visitors like this every day. Jessie stepped back and smiled, then walked to her car and climbed in.

As she drove off, Dog chased after the car, waving in excitement. Bill watched, shaking his head and smirking at Dog. He felt his heart palpitate a little too quickly and a little too long. He put his hand to his chest and took a long slow breath. It had been a full day, overflowing with emotions both light and dark. His body tensed as the anger and rage overcame all other thoughts. Anger was far easier to deal with. He slowly walked back to the farmhouse.

Flower

CHAPTER 8
Another Visitor

Dog sat crossed leg on the floor in front of the couch and watched with interest as Bill rifled through a cupboard in the living room. Jessie's visit had left Bill feeling like a shaken snow globe. He hoped that the sentiment would somehow settle. He grunted with satisfaction as he dragged out an old box labeled *Memories*, rummaged some more, then pulled out an old VHS tape. Dog eyed him curiously as he walked to the TV, pushed the tape into the VCR, and then sat on the couch near Dog.

Jessie had reminded Bill of all he had lost, and it made him miss Eleanor more than he had for some time. Normally, you can avoid the ghosts of the past if you busy yourself with the mundane tasks of today, but on this evening, there was no escape. He pressed play and absentmindedly scratched Dog's head

Bill's insides seized as Eleanor's voice, always full of fun and mischief, filled the room. "I was pretty angry when Bill said he was too tired to go out tonight." A crowd in the background laughed and cheered.

The slightly shaky handheld video zoomed in on Eleanor, with long sandy brown hair that fell to her shoulders, a weather-worn face, and eyes that danced with unbounded youthfulness that she never lost to her last breath. A younger Bill stood next to her, not a whisker in sight, and the lines not so deeply etched in his face than the Bill of this night.

Geez I had much more hair up top, Bill thought ruefully.

The younger Bill and Eleanor stood behind a large white cream frosted cake with 20 in bold blue numbers written across it. On-screen and off-screen they were surrounded by friends. Eleanor continued, "I figured, it was a good 20 years while it lasted."

Bill looked at his wife adoringly and laughed, along with the surrounding crowd.

"Then I came home to this!" The crowd whistled and cheered while Bill grinned. "I'm so lucky to be here with my friends and family. Wait, where's my baby girl?" she cried.

The cameraman whipped the camera around and caught a young lady shaking her head as she coyly wiped her long blonde hair from her face. Bill's gruff voice could be heard off-camera, "Come on, get over here."

The young lady walked up and stood beside Eleanor. "You'll always be our baby," she exclaimed as she drew her in for a big hug as the crowd cheered once more.

Dog's eyes lit up as he pointed to the screen. "Jessie?"

"Nah." Bill shook his head. "It's her mother, Mary."

Eleanor speaks again, "The only thing that could make this moment more perfect, is dessert!" Laughter erupted from the TV.

Bill's anger had once again consumed him. He paused the video with the remote. It froze on a shot of him hugging his wife, his daughter clapping beside him. The family is beaming from ear to ear.

"She never listened to a damn thing I said. I warned her about that man.

She let him destroy the family."

Dog whined sensing Bill's pain. Bill rose from the lounge, and Dog looked up at him concerned.

"Broke her mother's heart," Bill continued with much agitation.

Bill slowly made his way out of the room, his voice trailed off… "I knew best."

Bill slammed the door and could no longer be heard. Dog grunted softly, turned off the TV, and made his way from the farmhouse to the barn.

Dog entered the barn and closed the doors behind him, then crossed the room and turned on the lights. The soft glow of the fairy lights brought him a little comfort. He didn't like seeing Pa so upset. He picked up the turntable's arm and placed the needle on a record, but paused. The sound of the wind chimes dancing caught his attention. Dog began to sniff the air, it was the same scent he had caught the other night, something strange yet something oddly familiar.

He looked over at the open window but then returned his focus to the record player and dropped the needle on the record. John Farnham's "Chain Reaction" began to tinkle through the speakers. He climbed onto the bed and sat looking out the window, tapping to the beat on the window frame. Dog sniffed the air. There it was again. It smelt like himself—sort of. Confusion creased his forehead. He sniffed his own armpits just to be sure.

When he looked up again his whole body froze. Standing at the window was a Sasquatch who was also sniffing the air. Dog's eyes were wide as he inhaled deeply and took the creature in. Another Sasquatch just like him. No. Not like him. A female. She was slightly shorter and a little less stocky than Dog, with wispy fur that was a fairer auburn than his own.

Dog stopped sniffing… and breathing. He stared into her iridescent amber eyes. He could hear the music playing and the chimes tinkling, but at the same time he was aware of nothing. He sat transfixed. His bed burst into a rainbow of colorful flowers all around him, but he didn't notice. He tilted his head slowly to the side. He didn't know what to do.

He found his voice. "H… h… hel… lo?"

The female Sasquatch drew her eyes to a slit and growled low and fearfully, then dashed away from the window, toppling over nearby crates in her haste. The crashing of wood broke Dog's spell, and he jumped up.

"Lady!" he cried as he leaped through the window. He landed nimbly on the ground and gave chase.

Dog ran to the side of the barn only to find the crates sprawled across the ground. He urgently sniffed the air and turned to see the female running in the back fields toward the woods.

He raced after her. His chest pounding. His sturdy legs stomping the earth. He stopped as he reached the outer midfield and anxiously looked back at the farm. Pa's voice rang through his head, *No woods*. He turned toward the female, in the distance, he saw her disappear into the tree line. He took a deep breath, then continued, drawing ever closer to the edge of the words.

His feet became less sure, his heart wavered as he reached the fence. Dog stopped and stared, the silhouettes of the trees menacingly towered over him as they creeped and crawled into black nothingness. He paced back and forth, along the edge of the property staring at the farmhouse then back into the woods. He mumbled and grumbled to himself unsure.

A roar from deep within the woods echoed across the night, and Dog stopped still. His heart beat faster, and he whimpered softly, turned on his heels, and ran full speed to the safety of his barn, never looking back. Not once.

CHAPTER 9
Distracted

The morning sun peeked over the farm; birds hopped along the dewy grass, pecking for breakfast. The sunlight poured in through the barn window. Dog lay asleep snoring gently. The previous night's events had caused him much duress, and he'd tossed and turned all night, but he had finally managed to slip into some sort of a slumber an hour or so earlier. A rooster crowed in the distance. Dog's eyes snapped open, and he sprung straight up in bed and looked out the window toward the woods. He stared for a long moment remembering his visitor—her smell, her face, the way she moved. His heartbeat surged and his thoughts tumbled and jumped. Another of his kind. He had never even imagined that this could be possible. This Sasquatch had never been so excited before in his life—even more so than any *Los Pecados De Los Santos* series cliffhanger.

Dog snorted, jumped out of bed, and quickly pulled on his overalls and boots. He walked out of the barn to the back door of the farmhouse.

He was about to go in, but stopped short with his hand on the doorknob. He turned toward the woods. He placed his hands on his hips. He grumbled to himself, let go of the nob, and walked away from the house; he had some investigating to do. Dog was normally a calm soul, life on the farm was more often than not mellow, routine. But this morning, well…

He approached the toppled-over crates outside the barn, picked one up and smelt it with interest. The strong scent of his fellow Sasquatch tickled his nose hairs and soothed him like no other smell he could remember. He looked to the woods again hoping to see her one more time, but returned to the stack when all he saw were trees. He tidied up the other crates sprawled across the ground, carefully restacking them. Under one of the crates, he uncovered a Sasquatch footprint in the mud. He put his own foot next to it and grunted with interest at the similar size and shape. Dog quickly picked up some other crates and discovered more tracks. He glanced over at the farmhouse then back to the prints, then he let out a little confused moan and started to kick dirt over them to cover them up. He stared at the woods again and let out a small whine.

A short while later, Bill stepped out of the back door with his morning coffee in hand and in his other hand he held a deep brown Outback leather hat exactly like the one on his own head. He knew that Dog had been eyeing his hat for some time now and though he wasn't normally sentimental, this being Dog's birthday, or least the day he brought him home from the woods, he wanted to give him a little surprise. Bill stopped at the back steps and did a double-take. Dog was already up and mowing the lawn of all things. He sipped his coffee as he watched Dog steer the ride-on lawnmower along the fence line surrounding the property. Dog did a U-turn, then drove in the opposite direction, managing to maintain a straight line, all the while having his eyes locked on the tree line of the woods.

Bill frowned to himself. "What on earth?" he mumbled.

"Dog!" he called out, but Dog didn't hear him as he continued to ride along the fence. Bill put his fingers in his mouth and whistled loud and clear. Dog's head snapped to attention, and he saw Bill at the farmhouse. He swung the mower around and drove it back toward the barn while Bill walked up to meet him with a puzzled look.

As Dog climbed off the lawnmower, Bill handed him the hat. "Got you something," he said through a curious half-smile.

Excited, Dog took the hat and put it on his head. "Gift!" he cried.

Bill smiled. "Looks good." Dog eyes looked up at his hat, but he can only see the brim.

Bill nodded toward the mower. "Why are you mowing the lawn? Doesn't need it."

Dog anxiously looked at Bill, then removed his hat and nibbled gently on the brim.

"That's not food, Dog," Bill chided shaking his head.

Dog sheepishly removed the hat from his mouth and put it back on his head to cover his eyes. He stood still and held his breath. Bill looked at him for a moment perplexed then shook his head.

"Come on," he said, getting back to business. "Only two days till the fair. You've got pumpkin work, then we gotta load the truck."

Dog snorted in reluctant agreement as he followed Bill over to the pumpkin patch giving another long look to the woods.

Later that morning, Dog stood with his hands on his burgeoning pumpkin, but his eyes were on the woods. Bill walked by carrying a box of produce, once again puzzled by Dog's distraction.

"You better watch what you're doing, you don't want to crack it," he said over his shoulder as he headed to the truck.

Dog quickly nodded, grunted, and refocused on his task. He knew he had worked too hard to mess up the pumpkin this year.

After a quick lunch, Dog and Bill were loading boxes of produce from the barn into the back of the truck, Dog carried three to Bill's one.

"We've had three new orders this week," Bill said to Dog as he passed him.

Dog didn't respond. He was lost deep in thought, preoccupied with the woods. Dog lifted his boxes onto the back of the truck and spun around, something had caught his eye. He stared as a crow called in the distance then soared above the mouth of the woods. Dog's face slumped in disappointment, but he stood, watching intently, just in case.

"Two restaurants and a supermarket," Bill continued as he carried his box out of the barn to find Dog staring out at the woods again.

"What's the matter, boy?" he asked as he put his box on the back of the truck, but was met by silence. "Hey! What's the matter?" Bill said louder as he clapped his hands.

Dog snapped out of his gaze and looked at Bill with his eyes wide with fear as he considered his response. His super-sensitive hearing picked up a welcome distraction, the sound of a car approaching. He turned and pointed in excitement. "Jessie!"

Before Bill could speak, Jessie's car appeared in the distance and drove up to their truck. Dog bounded up to her door as she stepped out of the vehicle.

"Hey, Dog. Happy birthday!" Jessie said joyfully as she reached out and gave him a hug.

"Hat," said Dog as he pointed out Bill's gift to him on his head.

Jessie giggled as she stepped back to admire the new accessory. "Is that from Pa? Nice!" she said, smiling at Pa.

Dog tilted his head up, smiling as he looked at the brim.

"Hey, Pa," said Jessie as she walked over to Bill and gave him a hug too.

"Morning," said Bill with genuine warmth.

Jessie turned back to Dog. "Can I get a hand with these groceries?" she asked as she moved to the car. She stopped to give Dog a rub on the back and giggled, still so excited to discover a Sasquatch in the family; then walked to her car and popped the trunk.

"I thought you were bringing cake?" queried Bill when he saw a number of burgeoning shopping bags.

"I did, but I saw you needed a few extra supplies," Jessie shrugged.

Bill smiled and nodded with gratitude; he could see it was in her nature to look after people, just like her grandmother, and it was a new sensation to once again feel a little looked after.

Dog absentmindedly picked up several brown paper bags at once. The crash of a bag hitting the ground made Pa jump and he saw that once again his focus on the woods was to blame.

"Dog!" he said exasperated. "Where's your head?"

Dog quickly kneeled down and picked up the bag. Jessie was confused by the tension. "It's okay, Pa, it was just an accident."

Bill's nose flared. "He's distracted with the blasted woods." He looked at Dog suspiciously. "What's got you so interested?"

Dog put his head down and didn't respond. Bill was cranky. Not because of a dropped bag but his fear—fear that Dog may venture out into an unsafe world. He needed him to be as scared as he was.

"You know better, no woods!" he scolded.

Dog still said nothing. He just kept his head down; he sensed Pa's motivation. He was scared himself, but he still had to resist every urge to look at the woods again. Every urge. But there was someone like him out there. Just like him.

"Pa, can you please grab the last bag?" Jessie asked as she headed toward the house, trying to diffuse the awkwardness.

"Come on, Dog," she said sweetly as he gladly followed behind.

Jessie and Dog placed their shopping bags on the kitchen countertop. "Thanks, Dog." She smiled at him as she started to put the various items away. As Bill entered the kitchen with his bag, Jessie looked over at him.

"Mom had a bad night last night," she informed him.

Bill placed his bags on the countertop, his heart twinged, but he didn't say anything.

"She's finding it hard to sleep," Jessie said looking at him, wanting, hoping for any sort of breakthrough.

Bill started unpacking the groceries, but still didn't respond, his anger at his daughter and his desire not to upset Jessie rendered him speechless.

Jessie turned to the cupboard and stacked some tins not wanting him to see her face crumbling in hurt. She knew he was a hard man, but she didn't want to go through this alone; she was scared, and she could feel the panic rising. In an effort to change the subject, Jessie took a deep breath and walked to the counter to pull out a bright pink cake box from one of the shopping bags and placed it on the kitchen table.

"Dog, I've got something for you."

Dog stopped rifling through one of the other shopping bags and quickly went over to investigate the box. He gave it a little poke. "Gift?" he said as he scrunched his face in confusion.

Jessie flipped open the lid of the box and with a flourish of her hands revealed a large, family-sized vanilla cream cake with *Happy Birthday Dog* written on top in big bold red icing, spotted all over with red flowers.

"Birthday cake!" Jessie cried as she beamed at him.

Dog's jaw dropped as he stood frozen with eyes wide open. His mouth began to salivate as his hand slowly crept up to grab the cake.

"No, Dog," Bill shouted across the room, frightening Dog who quickly withdrew his hand. He looked at Bill sheepishly.

Jessie laughed and folded down the sides of the cake box. "Hold on, it's missing one thing," Jessie said gleefully.

She pulled a box of sparklers out of the shopping bag and stuck one into the cake, then lit it up. Dog took a hesitant step backward from the hiss of the sparkler as it caught fire. Jessie took his hand and pulled him back reassuringly.

"You're a grown man now, Dog," she said softly.

Dog was captivated by the shower of sparkles. He grinned with happiness as he admired the cake.

"Shiny!" he whispered in wonderment.

Dog was so enamored he didn't hear the pickup truck that pulled to a stop outside Bill's house. Ed stepped out and looked curiously at Jessie's car parked in the driveway, as he knew Bill didn't normally have visitors. In fact, never. He scanned the farm left and right, looking for Bill or the ginormous mutt. He heard laughter coming from the farmhouse. He raised a quizzical eyebrow as he walked to the back of his truck, reached into the tray to retrieve a chainsaw. He was headed toward the house when his phone rang, he pulled it out of his pocket and answered.

"Hello?" said Ed gruffly.

As Ed listened, his face creased with concern as this was a call he was hoping wouldn't come. More laughter rang from inside the farmhouse, so he walked in the opposite direction, his frustration growing. Ed stood beside the barn looking across at Bill's flourishing fields. He couldn't help but feel a pang of envy—his crops were doing great this year. He returned his focus to the conversation at hand.

"I'm filling an order next week, I'll be able to make my repayment then," Ed said with as much calm as he could muster. He nodded as the person on the other line spoke, "Yeah, I understand this is the last time. Appreciate it, Kevin," he said somberly.

He hung up and stared at his phone. The debt was closing in on him, and he could feel the panic rise in his chest. Hip hip hooray. Hip hip hooray! Came the cheer from the farmhouse. Ed turned and scowled at the farmhouse, with chainsaw still in hand he walked determinedly up the back porch steps.

Inside, Jessie and Dog were wearing party hats and despite his protests, Bill was too. Jessie clapped with excitement. "It's time to cut the cake and make a wish." She handed Dog a knife. Dog had seen this on TV, he stood poised to cut the cake, but stopped as his face clouded with anger. He let out a low growl.

"What's wrong?" Jessie asked, concerned.

"We've got a visitor," said Bill knowingly.

KNOCK. KNOCK. Bill removed his party hat. "Come on in, Ed," he called out.

Ed entered the kitchen holding the chainsaw. "Hey. Just returning your..."

He stopped in his tracks when he saw Jessie standing next to Dog. Jessie stared at the visitor who had an air of gruffness about him. She smiled uneasily.

"You remember my granddaughter, Jessie," said Bill.

Ed placed the chainsaw on the kitchen counter. "Gosh, you've grown, I wouldn't have recognized you."

"Oh… Ed. Yes, it's been a long time," Jessie happily replied.

"Your dad still around? He owes me for some work I did on his car," Ed said matter-of-factly.

Jessie's face burned red as she averted her eyes.

Bill saw his granddaughter's shame and jumped in. "He's not, and that's not Jessie's business," he said firmly.

"Oh, that's fine" Jessie replied. "We're just having a birthday party for Dog. Cake?" she offered, trying to diffuse the situation.

Ed couldn't contain his disdain at the scene in front of him and rolled his eyes. "Now I've seen it all. No thanks."

There was silence, Dog looked angrily at Ed. Bill just sighed. He was used to Ed and his antics. Jessie stood wide-eyed feeling the intense awkwardness fill the room.

"I lost six chickens last night," Ed stated to Bill.

Bill frowned. "They get out?"

Ed shook his head angrily. "Looks like a wild animal broke into the coop," he said as he looked at Dog suspiciously. "Seen any around?"

Dog growled under his breath and took a defensive stance, backing away slightly.

Bill spun to face Dog. "Dog! Go put the chainsaw in the barn." He knew he had to diffuse the situation, and this was the easiest way to do that.

Dog snorted and picked up the chainsaw. Jessie felt bad for him. "Here, take some cake with you." Jessie handed him a huge wedge of cake on a paper plate. He grinned at her gratefully, picked up the chainsaw, and walked to the door, but not before exchanging a glare with Ed as he exited the room.

Jessie stood awkwardly and not knowing what else to do, she put a large piece of cake into her mouth. Bill looked at his neighbor with concern; his disdain for Dog had grown throughout the years, but he wanted to keep the peace.

"Probably just a coyote. I'll keep an eye out," said Bill.

Ed looked at Bill as he narrowed his eyes. "Do that. I can't afford to lose any more. They pay my bills." A pained expression flashed on his face as he quickly looked down.

Bill stared at him intently. "Everything okay, Ed?" he asked.

Ed snorted, annoyed at himself for even bringing it up. "Yeah. Just trying to keep my head above water," he muttered.

Jessie watched them both feeling uneasy. All she could do was keep shoveling cake into her mouth. She couldn't remember a time when she had been in such an uncomfortable predicament.

Bill nodded in sympathy. "Yeah. I get it."

Ed jerked his head up and looked Bill square in the eyes, "Do you, Bill? You seem to be doing okay with your organic certification."

Bill was hit by a wave of guilt. It was his turn to hang his head. Jessie's eyes widened with the realization that Ed had no idea about Dog's connection to nature; the only thing she could do was eat more cake.

Dog had exited through the front door of the farmhouse and began to walk down the porch steps, but he stopped in his tracks when he saw a box of apples spilled onto the ground near the back of their truck. He sniffed the air but could not detect anything on the wind. He quickly retreated back inside the farmhouse and watched with interest through the screen door.

He could hear the others talking inside, but he focused intently on the truck and barn as he shoveled cake into his mouth. His mouth salivated with the pure bliss of the sugar and cream overload. The wind chimes tinkled from across the barn as a gentle breeze picked up. Dog sniffed the air with growing excitement and chills rippled all over his body with anticipation.

Still holding the chainsaw and plate of cake, he opened the back door and, with trepidation, he stepped gingerly down the porch steps once more. Quickly and quietly, he snuck toward the truck. Dog stood stiffly near the front of the vehicle. He could hear someone rummaging through the boxes of apples on the back. Dog cautiously looked through the windshield, but the stacked produce boxes blocked his view.

He crept along the side of the vehicle and peered around the back of the truck to see the female Sasquatch standing there eating an apple. She stopped mid-bite and sniffed the air. Dog took a nervous breath and then stepped into her view. He was still holding the chainsaw and cake, wearing the party hat, and had whipped cream smeared all around his mouth.

The two Sasquatches looked at each other intently sniffing the air softly. Unsure of how to proceed, Dog decided to use his manners and politely held out the plate. "Cake?" he offered.

The female Sasquatch's eyes flashed with confusion and she growled loudly at Dog. This, in turn, startled Dog who dropped the chainsaw and plate in fright. The clunk and clank frightened her even further and she growled louder.

In the background, the back door of the farmhouse slammed shut. "Just keep an eye on your Dog," Ed could be heard.

"Jesus, Ed, the only time he eats chicken is if it's extra crispy, from a bucket," Bill responded with exasperation.

Dog looked past the truck to see Ed and Bill walking toward them. Panic seized him as he raised a finger to his mouth. "Shh," he whispered.

His gesture only agitated the Sasquatch further, she looked up at his party hat all bright and pink and sparkling and continued to growl. Dog realized he was still wearing the party hat and quickly removed it.

"Hey, looks like one of your boxes has come off the truck," Ed could be heard saying.

Dog peeked around the truck to see Ed pointing his way, he quickly ducked out of view.

"Dog?" called Bill.

Dog nervously looked around, not sure of what to do. He took a few steps toward the barn. "Barn," he whispered urgently to the female, waving for her to go inside. The female stood her ground and continued to growl.

Dog hurriedly shuffled back to the truck and took another peek at Bill and Ed—they were now almost upon them. He stepped out from behind the truck in an attempt to block their view of the female.

Bill frowned as he surveyed the toppled crates and apples strewn all over the ground. "Dog, what's happened here?"

Dog looked anxiously at Bill and Ed but didn't respond.

Bill went to step around Dog, but Dog took a step in front of him, cutting him off. Bill stopped and looked up at Dog clearly annoyed.

"What are you doing? Out of the way."

Bill pushed past him, and Dog held his breath as he spun around. Bill walked to the back of the truck to find the chainsaw and plate on the ground, along with a mess of cake and apples.

Dog slowly exhaled, relieved to discover the female had vanished. He sniffed the air furiously as his eyes darted around looking for her. Bill bent down and picked up a half-eaten apple, he looked at Dog incredulously.

"What's gotten into you?"

Dog didn't respond, but had a guilty look on his face.

Ed shook his head. "Looks like you've got yourself a discipline problem," he scoffed barely unable to contain his disgust. "I best be off so you can deal with it," he said as he turned and left for his truck.

Bill watched him leave with a frown growing ever deeper masking his underlying shame. "Clean up this mess," he snapped and walked off shaking his head.

Dog was quick to comply and started picking up the apples from the ground. Jessie wandered over. She felt sorry for Dog, so bent down and helped by picking up the plate and scooping up the cake.

"I saved you a big piece inside," she said to Dog, who replied with a troubled grunt.

On any given day, Dog's focus would have been farming, television, and eating as many treats as he could stomach—the latter taking precedence. Now he couldn't think of anything but a certain female Sasquatch. He could smell her on the crate and on the apples. Everywhere. He looked around carefully so as not to raise suspicion, wondering where she had gone and when he would see her again. Not even the promise of cake ladened with cream could distract him. His priorities had definitely shifted.

CHAPTER 10
Moment of Freedom

An hour or so later, the truck was loaded. Dog put a lid on the last apple box andt flipped shut the truck's tailgate, then walked around to the driver's side. Bill leaned out the window and looked intently at Dog—he'd often left him alone on the farm, but today he felt unsure, even though Jessie was there. He couldn't shake the feeling that Dog was acting weird. Bill remembered adolescence and wondered whether Sasquatches experience teenage hormone changes too.

Bill checked his watch. He needed to get this delivery done now if he wanted to be back before dark. "Don't waste your day playing with Jessie. Get your chores done," he said.

Dog nodded and waved as he watched Bill drive off. As soon as he was out of sight, Dog wasted no time and ran into the barn. He sniffed the air and looked around frantically, but couldn't find the female Sasquatch.

He kneeled on his bed and looked out the window at the woods; he sighed sadly.

Jessie followed him into the barn. "Hey, Dog!" she chirped. Dog jumped in fright. "Didn't mean to scare you," she giggled. Jessie sat next to him on the bed and looked out at the woods, then back at Dog. She frowned. "What ya looking at?" Dog just grunted softly. "You've never been off the farm, have you?" she asked softly.

Dog shook his head. She looked at him with pity, such a magnificent creature who was born to roam wild and free, and here he was stuck on a farm. A plan started to form in her mind. A little road trip should be fine if she were careful. Pa would never know. She looked at her watch—they'd have to be quick.

"Why don't I take you out for a drive… for your birthday." Her eyes glistened with excitement.

Dog recoiled. He was not allowed off the farm and had no desire to know Pa's wrath. He shook his head firmly.

Jessie nodded in understanding. "Don't worry about Pa. We'll be home before he gets back," she said reassuringly.

Dog shook his head again, his eyes wide with fear, but his heart longed to see what lay beyond the fence of Jackson Farm.

Jessie saw a hint of a budge in Dog's eyes. She really believed that a trip off the farm would be the best experience ever for Dog, so she was not going to give up. What Pa didn't know wouldn't hurt him.

"Come on, it'll be our secret," she whispered.

Dog's head perked up. "Secret?" he whispered back with a slight smile.

Jessie's tiny Toyota hurtled down an otherwise deserted highway. She looked over from behind the wheel at the Sasquatch crammed into the passenger seat and smiled as her heart warmed with joy. Dog had his head out the window as the wind hit him full force in the face.

He loved it—it made him feel more alive than he had ever known possible. ACDC blasted through the car speakers as they both sang the letters of the song's title "TNT" at the top of their voices. Up ahead, Jessie saw a car approaching.

"Dog. Come back inside," she called over the music, turning the volume down. Dog pulled his head in quickly.

The other car whizzed by as they both kept their eyes forward trying not to look suspicious. She wasn't sure what she would say if they got pulled over, but she had told Dog to sit and say nothing and nod sometimes. She figured she would say something about a fancy dress party.

"You having fun?" she asked.

Dog happily nodded.

"Good. I think you're gonna like where I'm taking you," she said as she turned the volume back up. Dog stuck his head back out the window as Jessie's car sped into the distance.

Jessie and Dog sat side-by-side on a large rock, spread before them was the national forest, a panoramic spread of luscious evergreen as far as the eye could see.

"Isn't it beautiful?" Jessie whispered.

Dog stared in awe. His world view had consisted of the fifty acres or so of Jackson Farm, and he knew every inch of that land, every plant, every tree. He had often thought of what lay beyond the farm fence—the world he had seen on TV. He could always smell it, taste it on the wind, but he had never touched it. His fear of the world had never let him experience it for real.

"The farm is just over that way," Jessie continued as she pointed, "and all those trees, that's the woods… where you came from."

Dog looked out attentively as they sat together in silence, soaking in the gloriousness and both feeling so small in the face of it.

Jessie studied Dog out of the corner of her eye. Finally, she said, "Dog, there's such a big world out there… you must be lonely on the farm with just Pa."

"Pa," Dog repeated, still looking over the forest view.

She continued, "You and me, we're kind of the same. I've only got Mom."

Dog snapped at a fly in the air. Jessie wasn't sure if he was listening or even understood, but she went on. "When she got sick, I realized how important family was. I'm glad I have you and Pa in my life now."

"Family," Dog said.

Jessie squeezed his knee. As soon as she was old enough, she had taken off backpacking around the world to escape their family drama. But as soon as she got the call that her mother was sick, she jumped on the first plane home. When she saw how ill her mother was, she knew she had to reach out to her grandfather. He had been cut-off and angry for so long. He was gruff, but she remembered his kindness and how much he had loved her and looked after her, especially when things got really bad between her parents. She was glad she had reached out because she would never have met such an extraordinary creature.

Dog and Jessie soaked in the beauty of the landscape. The air was still, and crows called far in the distance. Jessie looked at Dog again. She wondered about him; how lonely he must be. At least she had a family, despite how messy and broken hers was. Could he be the only Sasquatch in the world?

"I wonder if there's any more like you out there?" she asked curiously.

Dog turned to Jessie with wide eyes in shock. He was about to say something, but thought better of it and just grunted and returned his gaze to the woods.

Jessie frowned at Dog thoughtfully. He was wearing his suspicious poker face, the same kind of face that he wore when he played snap. Was he hiding something?

"What?" she queried.

Without turning, Dog shook his head then kept his focus forward still with his poker face. Jessie's mouth dropped.

"There's more like you out there?" she asked, fully knowing the answer—of course there were. It's biology. He had to come from somewhere.

Dog merely grunted and shrugged.

"Dog?" she prodded gently.

Dog still kept his eyes straight ahead while he considered her question. Jessie could see that he was scared and confused; she took him by the hand.

Earnestly and softly she spoke, "You can tell me."

Dog looked at their hands and nodded slowly.

Jessie's eyes opened wide. "How do you know?"

Dog kept his head down. "Lady," he barely whispered.

"What do you mean? You've seen a female Sasquatch?" Jessie's voice jumped an octave.

Dog nodded timidly. His large bulking muscle. His face rugged and lined. She reasoned he must be at an age where male Sasquatches start thinking about female Sasquatches.

Her heart jumped with excitement, and she broke into a huge grin. She couldn't contain her excitement and punched him on the arm.

"Wow, you've got a girlfriend!"

Dog shook his head sadly. "No."

Jessie stopped, unsure of what he meant. "She's not your friend?"

"Scare," Dog mumbled.

Jessie frowned, confused. "You're scared of her?"

Dog shook his head.

Jessie sat for a moment as she looked at Dog. She took in his overalls, his hat, his shoes. She remembered reading about animals from the wild that rejected other animals that had been held in captivity and then released back into their natural habitat—rejected because they were different.

Her mind raced excited at piecing together the puzzle. "She's scared of you! Of course, you live like a human, and she's from the woods," she said as she teasingly tugged at his denim overalls.

Dog looked down at his clothes as he slowly began to understand how she could indeed be scared of him.

"What happened?" Jessie said softly.

"Talk," Dog replied.

Jessie thought for a moment as she tried to decipher the Sasquatch code. Talk? Talk… She thought, then nodded to herself with a smile. "What did you say?"

Dog cringed at the memory. "Hello."

Jessie slapped her forehead—now the dilemma was clear. "You can't say 'hello.' You need to speak like a Sasquatch."

She smiled sadly. He was so busy trying to be a human that he had lost the ability to be his own kind. Pa meant well, but this magnificent being had no idea how to be what he was supposed to be.

Dog sat in silence, utterly perplexed. He could barely speak human, so how would he ever know how to speak Sasquatch? He looked out at the forest that stretched at their feet—she was out there somewhere. He wanted to see her again more than he could describe in any sound or language.

Jessie was also lost in thought but was becoming even more excited. "Come on. What would a Sasquatch say?"

Dog whimpered in response and bowed his head.

"Go on. Don't be shy," Jessie pushed his arm lovingly.

Dog hesitated for a moment then attempted to roar, but sounded more like a teenage boy whose voice is breaking, or perhaps being strangled. Dog grunted and frowned with embarrassment.

"That's good, Dog, but do it from here," Jessie laughed as she gave his chest a big thump. "Let me show you," she took a deep breath, then bellowed and roared with all her might. It echoed from the mountain, and Jessie laughed hard as Dog also guffawed to see a human try to be a Sasquatch. "Not exactly right," she giggled, "but you see what I mean. Take a deep breath, then roar."

Dog gave it another go. He breathed deep. "Rooaarr!"

This time he sounded like a teenage goose being throttled, but Jessie was getting excited. She could see the emotion was there. He wanted to roar like any beast of the wild.

"Stronger, Dog. Louder," she cried. "Use your voice. Then call to her, across the forest. Let her know you are here."

"ROOAARR!"

Jessie jumped up and clapped once again. There was still a long way to go, but this was the closest he had been to a Sasquatch in his entire life. Jessie cupped her hands to her face and roared again. Dog joined her and they called and roared across the forest, not really improving but feeling the utter joy of this rare moment of freedom.

They roared themselves hoarse, and finally, they both broke down laughing. "Oh well. It's a good start," Jessie croaked. "Just keep practicing."

Dog nodded and looked out over the endless view of trees. All of which was supposed to be his world, but it was a world that terrified him and was as foreign to him as any planet in outer space.

Jessie pulled out her phone to check the time. "Come on, we better head back," she said sadly.

As Dog reluctantly started to walk back to the car, he took one last longing look back over the forest; he could feel it calling, roaring back to him.

The car ride home was more of a solemn affair, as both Jessie and Dog were lost in their thoughts. As they approached the farm, they could see Bill standing by his truck outside the barn. He was home early and waiting for them to arrive. Jessie's heart sank.

"Oh no," she whispered as Dog whimpered. Jessie took a deep breath. "It's okay. I'm sure it'll be fine." Dog looked at her painfully, sensing her lie.

Bill stood fuming as he watched Jessie park behind his truck. Before she had even gotten out of the car, Bill wasted no time setting upon her.

"Are you out of your mind?" he barked.

Jessie and Dog stepped out of the car. Dog stayed on his side and looked down in shame as Bill focused his anger on Jessie.

"You had no right taking Dog off the farm."

"It was just a harmless drive," Jessie offered, trying to diffuse the situation. "Nobody saw us, it's fine."

"Do you have any idea what would happen if he were discovered?" Bill bellowed incredulously. All of his worst fears over the years fueled his anger.

Jessie looked at her raging grandfather and understood, but was also annoyed that he had no idea what Dog needed. "Pa, he's an adult now. You can't keep him locked up on the farm forever. He comes from the woods, he should have a little freedom."

Dog's head lifted with interest when he heard Jessie's words. Freedom. This was a new word, and he liked how that felt, smelled, and tasted.

Bill frustratingly dismissed her with a hand wave. "He's domesticated; he wouldn't last an hour out there." His eyes narrowed. "I'll decide what's best for Dog, not you."

Jessie shook her head with her own frustration. "I'm just saying, you need to give him a cha—"

"You're just like your mother," Bill yelled, his face seething red. "You don't listen to a damn thing."

Jessie inhaled a breath sharply as rage overran her mind. "Really?" she took a step forward and stared him down. "So you going to cut me off now?"

Dog watched both of them with a horrible tension filling his belly.

It was pouring out of Bill now—the years, the resentment, the bitterness. "Your mother made her choice when she stuck by your good-for-nothing father!"

Jessie shook her head. "It was never just about him. You tried to control everything she did. They were her mistakes to make, and you should have loved her no matter what." Jessie got into her car and slammed the door.

She opened the window and glared at him more, not finished. "I came here to try and mend the years, but you make it impossible to let anyone in. Dog's the only one left who cares about you." She started the engine. She was breathing heavily and was so very angry. She had years of frustration buried inside her as well.

"You better treat him with respect, or he'll leave you just like Mom did," she reversed fast as Dog stepped out of the way.

He was speechless. Bill's eyes went dark as he watched her speed off.

"Jessie?" Dog moaned, distressed at all the yelling, all the anger. His first taste of freedom had quickly spoiled and soured.

Bill turned to Dog. "Get in the barn. You can spend the rest of the day in there."

Dog didn't move, he just stood staring straight at his Pa. Anger welled in him. This had been one of the best days of his life. All he had ever known was this farm, and now he saw the world a whole lot differently.

"Did you hear me? Get," Bill said, annoyed.

Dog stood tall and spoke with a firm voice, "No."

Bill's eyes widened as his anger surged. "What did you say?"

They stared each other down. *Damn Jessie*, Bill thought, *putting ideas inside his head. How could he live any other way now?* A pang of guilt hit him. He knew that he hadn't shown Dog how to survive in the wild. He had raised him human, which was all the more reason now that he had to protect him. Bill's anger peaked. He had to protect him.

"Get in the barn right now!" he said, barely containing his fury.

Dog looked at Pa and a shot of fear rose in him. He had been taught about respect from an early age. He knew that Pa was the most important thing in the world to him. He could see the old man, red and raging, and he just wanted all the fighting to stop. He gave a grunt, turned heel, and ran to the barn.

Bill watched him go, shaken to the core. He shook his head and dejectedly walked back to the house.

Inside the barn, Dog paced back and forth. He clenched his fists by his sides as he grunted, mumbled, and growled angrily to himself. He was frustrated. Frustrated at everyone. Frustrated at Pa for keeping him on this farm. Frustrated at Jessie for showing him how much he was missing out on. Frustrated at them both for fighting and ruining his chance of having a family. Frustrated at the female Sasquatch for turning up and making him feel a way he had never felt before. Grrr. Grrr. Grrr.

After several laps of the room, he stopped at the window and looked out at the woods. But most all, he was frustrated at himself for not really being a Sasquatch and not really being a human.

He lay down on the bed and whined softly and sadly to himself.

Wither

CHAPTER 11
Closer

The full moon shone way up high in the heavens. A slightly snoring Dog was stirred by the gentle tinkle of his wind chimes blowing in the breeze. He bolted upright, looked out the window at the woods, and then snapped his head toward the farmhouse. The lights were off. He knew the rules. He knew what was expected of him and what the consequences would be if he were caught. He paused for a moment, but not a moment more and jumped out of bed.

A short while later, dressed in his overalls and boots, Dog stood by the wood's edge, staring into the darkness. He turned and looked back at the farmhouse, illuminated by the moon's glow. He took a deep breath, then entered the woods.

Dog sniffed the air as he walked through the trees. He nervously looked left and right, unsure and untrusting of his natural instinct. A choir of insects and strange woodland creatures echoed around him. He reached a clearing and stopped to smell the air, then tried calling for the female Sasquatch.

"Rooaarr."

It was weak and lacked confidence. Dog waited, not daring to breathe. Nothing. He frowned. He remembered Jessie's words, *feel it here,* and he pounded his chest and tried again.

"ROOAARR."

Better, but barely. Dog eagerly looked around for the female. Hoping.

Still nothing. His face slumped in disappointment. He took a deep breath before the sound could leave his mouth.

"ROOOAAARR!" The female Sasquatch's call reverberated through the trees, silencing the noisy insects and creatures.

Dog nervously looked around but heard nothing except his own rapid breath.

He felt the fear and panic rising. He had a change of heart and began to turn to leave. At that moment, the female Sasquatch appeared on the opposite side of the clearing.

Dog stopped in his tracks as they stared at each other, the insects resuming their song. An ascending din that electrified the night sky.

Dog's heart pounded in his ears and in his chest, and his mouth felt so dry. He didn't know what to do. He thumped his fist against his chest.

"Dog," he called, instantly regretting his decision.

The female growled almost dismissively and turned to leave. Dog's eyes darted as he tried to think of what to do. In a panic, he grunted loudly at her.

"GRRR."

The female stopped and turned around. Dog was surprised. His heart pounded; his body flooded with excitement. He was doing it. He grunted some more.

"GRR. GRRR. GRR."

He put how he felt into those sounds. How he wanted her to stay, how he thought she was amazing, how he thought he was the only one of his kind that existed, and how he felt so lonely. From deep inside, he expressed more in those few grunts than if he had strung together one hundred words. The most wonderful part of it all was that she seemed to understand.

The two Sasquatches began to circle the clearing sizing one another up-and-down, still keeping a wary distance. Dog caught her scent on the breeze, and his whole body was flooded with chills. The only point of reference he had was when Lucia meet Hernadez in *Los Pecados De Los Santos* and her whole world stopped and spun around her.

Dog stopped and faced the female. The female mirrored him.

With their eyes locked, Dog bent down on one knee and placed his palm on the ground. He smiled as delicate pink flowers began shooting up from the grass around them. Under the gaze of the full moon, the barren clearing slowly transformed into a luscious field of grass and blushing flowers.

The female smiled in appreciation as she kneeled to meet him at eye level. She too placed her palm on the ground and instantly a path of bold white flowers sprouted amongst the pink ones all the way to Dog's feet.

They both rose to their full height then walked across the path of flowers to meet each other in the middle. Dog wasn't sure if he had been breathing. He didn't remember how he had even got to be face-to-face with the most beautiful creature he had ever seen. He took in her dark auburn locks, the deep intensity of her brown eyes with startling amber flecks.

He breathed her in. It was the most comforting and intoxicating scent that nearly knocked him over with its earthiness. He felt desire; he wanted to know her. They stepped closer still and began to sniff one another all over their bodies before their eyes eventually locked once more. The female smiled and touched the back of her hand to Dog's temple. A charge of electricity, nature itself, jolted through his whole body.

He was entranced, he was smitten, he was…

SNAP.

Their tender moment was interrupted.

SNAP.

SNAP.

Someone was in the woods walking toward them.

Their other primal instinct took hold. In a panic, the female sniffed the air, without even a grunt to Dog, she fled into the woods. Dog also sniffed the air and growled to himself as he caught an all too familiar scent. Then he ran in the opposite direction as fast as his legs would carry him. His mind whirled with joy and fear.

Moments later, Ed, holding a shotgun, stepped out from the trees into the field of flowers. He scanned the area, then bent down and angrily plucked a flower from the ground. Ed snarled at it as his eyes once again scanned the perimeter. He looked at the flower, then crushed it in his fist and tossed it away before he too disappeared into the woods.

Bill sat on the couch, illuminated only by the light of the television. The same home movie that he watched the previous night was playing.

"Surprise!" the crowd cried in unison.

There was a ruckus of cheering, laughter, and applause as Bill smiled.

"My goodness… Bill, I'm going to kill you! Twenty years of marriage, I'll get less time for murder," Eleanor said, smirking.

The crowd roared with laughter.

Bill used the remote to pause the video. He smiled as he looked at the image of Eleanor beaming. His heart sank. He knew what she would do, what she would say if she could see him now. Just like all those times when she steered his course, and just like those times, he wouldn't want to hear it, but she'd make him listen anyway. Family was everything to her. Everything.

He sat quietly, looking at the freeze frame. So many years had passed, but tonight it felt like just yesterday. He reached into his shirt pocket and pulled out the hospital business card. He stared at it for a moment, his heart still frozen, but a little less cold. He threw all of that from his mind as he used the remote to turn off the TV. The room went dark.

He got up and headed toward the hallway, but stopped when something caught his eye outside the window.

Dog was entering the barn and then closed the door behind him. Bill was puzzled, wondering what he was up to. *He had probably heard a fox or something* he surmised, then continued on his way to bed without giving it another thought.

CHAPTER 12
Smoke and Mirrors

It was mid-morning, and on this chilly day the sun had only just begun to warm the earth. Ed strode across the back of his property with his cell phone to his ear; his work boots squelched determinedly in the wet morning grass. He followed a trail of chicken feathers to his chicken coops.

He had his cell phone to his ear and was trying to process the devastating news he was listening to on top of the foreboding sign of the strewn chicken feather path before him.

"Come on, Phil, you've been my customer for ten years," he pleaded, shaking his head. Fear seized his chest; this could sink his farm entirely.

Ed stopped and bent down to examine a clump of feathers as the caller spoke.

"No. Organic isn't economical for me," Ed said through gritted teeth. He seethed, the cost of getting an organic license far outweighed the financial benefit. He was organic anyway. He just couldn't afford the damn picture on the box.

He tossed the feathers angrily and stood up.

"Yeah, I know, it's just business," he sighed.

Ed continued following the feathers until he reached the chicken coop. He stopped and did a rough count of the chicken heads he saw. Five missing. He shook his head in frustration.

"Can I ask who your new supplier is?" His eyes narrowing with a growing level of rage.

He stepped into the coop as chickens scattered to reveal a large paw print in the dirt. Ed knew instantly it was the Sasquatch. He paused. He was seeing things more clearly than he ever had.

"That's fine, I'm pretty sure I know," he said with steely calmness.

He hung up the phone and kicked the Sasquatch print in anger, then turned heel and stormed across his property, heading in the direction of his nearest neighbor.

Kneeling in the dirt in front of his giant pumpkin, Dog worked his magic on several smaller pumpkins, which grew delightfully more plump and full with a deep orange shine. He threw his head back to observe his handiwork. Nearby, Bill kneeled by a wooden pallet hammering nails around the edge.

Bill looked up at Dog with a scowl then continued his angry hammering. He was still furious with Dog on account of his behavior yesterday and had been decidedly cool all morning. Dog glanced to his side, sensing the tension and thought it best to keep out of his way.

Ed made his way across the back of Jackson Farm and saw Bill and Dog as they worked in the distance. Bill's hammering echoed throughout the field, masking his approach from Dog's heightened senses. Ed continued out of sight. He made it to the side of the barn and peeked around the corner to watch them.

What he saw made his whole body freeze. He was sure his eyes were deceiving him. Had the beast just placed his hands on a small pumpkin and it grew? He looked again. God damn it, that thing grew. His mind felt like it was exploding into a thousand fragments, which he began to piece together. Ed had never understood how Bill's farm did so well, regardless of season and weather. He had never known why his friend of so many years averted eyes when he asked how he managed to do so well. His mind raced. Those blasted spring flowers that grew all over the forest even in the winter frost. God damn it, that grotesque creature made plants grow. The rage was too much to contain.

"Liars. Cheats. I knew something wasn't right!" Ed bellowed as Dog and Bill jumped to their feet and turned to see Ed. Bill knew this day would eventually arrive.

Bill's eyes widened in fear, and he took a few steps toward Ed, ensuring he stood between him and Dog. He knew Ed was a hothead, and this whole situation had the potential to get out of control quickly.

"Ed, I didn't know how to tell you. I was just… I was just trying to protect him," Bill tried to reason.

"Protect him?" Ed scoffed. "We've been friends for decades, yet you lie to me, steal my business, and your goddamned Sasquatch is stealing my chickens." Ed's red face sweated with anger and disbelief.

"Whoa, hold up there Ed. What do you mean I stole your business?"

"Ellis Foods?" Ed responded in a frustrated tone.

"We just got business from Inner Fresh, not Ellis—"

"They're the same people, Bill. They've gone organic," Ed roared with exasperation.

Bill's face jumped in surprise. "I'm sorry to hear it, Ed, but we have different businesses. I can't stop people from going organic."

Ed walked over to the giant pumpkin and waved his hand at it and Dog.

"You're all smoke and mirrors, Bill," he cried. "Your organic certification means nothing when he's behind it." He pointed accusingly at Dog, "And he attacked my coop again last night."

"I told you, Ed, Dog hasn't been stealing your chickens," Bill said, trying to remain calm.

"You're wrong," raged Bill. "He left footprints to prove it."

Dog growled low and angrily in the background. Bill turned his head and snapped at Dog, "Quiet."

Dog grumbled an annoyed incoherent word or two, but he obeyed and made no other sound.

Bill turned back to Ed. "I'm sorry that things are tough for you, but Dog never leaves the farm." His face twitched at that slight lie, remembering the night before. "And he's always in boots. Those prints… they probably belong to some other Sasquatch."

Dog's eyes widened and he whimpered slightly. Ed seized on it.

"Another Sasquatch, hey? I've spoken to Ted Jeffries. Proof of a real, live Bigfoot will sort out my money troubles. We kept this monster a secret to stop all the leeches from making our life a misery. And you know what? You're the worst leech of all, Bill. You've been profiting from it all along while the rest of us drown. Should've taken care of this years ago."

Dog growled once more, but this time it took a more menacing tone. Bill waved his hand to silence him.

"Ed—" Bill began, but he was cut off.

"I'm not gonna lose my farm over him. That's a promise." Ed spat.

"Don't do anything foolish," Bill warned. He knew he was losing control of this situation, and he was scared—he didn't know what Ed would do to save his farm.

Ed laughed cruelly, shook his head with disgust, then bent over and picked up the hammer sitting on the pallet. He swung wildly at the massive pumpkin.

WHACK.

A hole opened in the perfect orange shell. Dog roared and lunged at Ed, but Bill grabbed hold of Dog. Dog could have easily overpowered Bill and Ed both, but Bill had taught him long ago that nothing good ever came from violence.

The hole split open even wider. Dog sobbed deep in his throat.

"Stop," screamed Bill, but Ed paid no attention and swung his arm wildly.

WHACK.

This final blow cracked the pumpkin from top to bottom as seeds spilled from its guts.

Dog growled and whimpered. "It's okay, boy," he said trying to console him but shaking with his own rage. "It's okay."

Bill scowled at Ed. "You best leave," he roared. "Now!"

Ed stared Bill dead in the eyes. "If he steps one foot off this farm, he's mine." Ed threw the hammer on the ground and started walking toward his farm. He called over his shoulder tauntingly, "Sasquatch hunting season is open."

Dog ran over to his pumpkin. He dropped to his knees and placed his hands over the crack, growling at Ed as he walked away. Every part of him wanted to attack that horrible, nasty man who had been nothing but cruel to him his entire life. Despite what Bill had said, Dog was sure it would make him feel better. He felt a sob grow in his throat as he turned his attention back to the pumpkin. It was a disaster.

Bill angrily walked toward Dog and stood over him. He was in total shock, and his body shook from what had just occurred, but he still had many bones to pick with the young Sasquatch.

"What a mess," he said wearily as Dog desperately laid his hands on the shell trying to repair his beloved pumpkin, but nothing happened.

Bill continued in a serious low tone, "I saw you outside your barn last night." Dog did not dare look at him and just tended to his pumpkin. "Did you go to Ed's farm?" Bill asked his voice lower still, but a hint of frustration colored the words.

Dog stared at his pumpkin, hoping that if he said nothing Bill would just give up.

"Dog!" Bill raised his voice with irritation.

Dog shook his head, still not looking at him.

"Did you take his chickens?" he wanted to scream at him but tried to restrain himself.

"No," Dog said, annoyed to think Bill would think that.

Bill glared at Dog, his mind recalling something Ed had said. "Is there another Sasquatch out there?" he asked loud and clear. This would explain a lot about his recent behavior. Bill watched him like a hawk.

Dog dropped his hands for a moment, then raised them over the crack again, but said nothing.

Bill sighed. "Stand up, Dog," he said kindly but firmly.

Dog reluctantly stood. He had a guilty look on his face.

"Is there another Sasquatch out there?" Bill asked, looking him directly in the eyes.

Dog hesitated. He didn't want to lie or hide anything from Pa, but he needed to protect her.

"Dog?" Bill asked quietly.

Dog dropped his head. "Yes."

"God dammit," Bill griped as he took a step back. "I knew something was up with you."

"Friend," Dog offered in a pleading tone.

Bill pointed his finger angrily. "That thing is not your friend."

"Lady," Dog said sadly.

Bill paused and thought for a moment as his heart sank. "I know you'd like some company," he said with tenderness—after all, Bill knew how he'd felt when he lost his best friend in the world. "But Ed's after her, and there's nothing I can do to stop him. My job is to protect you."

Dog hung his head sadly. He didn't say anything. He was once again caught between his two worlds, and he didn't know which way to turn.

"She'll ruin your life, Dog," Bill warned. This female Sasquatch was wild. She was going to bring trouble into his life if he didn't stop it now. Bill knew he had to put fear in him; it was the only way. "Do you want scientists poking needles in you every day?" Bill warned. "And that's the best-case scenario. Ed's got nothing to lose. If he sees you out there…"

Dog let out a low growl, the mention of Ed filled him with instant boiling anger.

"Stay out of the woods Dog… you hear me?" Bill's voice was sharp and pointed. "Ed is a huntsman. He's gonna fill those woods with traps. You ain't safe."

Dog shrugged his shoulders. Bill was growing frustrated again.

"Don't make me chain you up, boy," he warned. "No woods, we clear?" Bill didn't want to threaten him with that, but he didn't know what else would get through to him.

Dog looked defeated and nodded.

Bill searched Dog's face and was satisfied. He turned to look at the pumpkin and frowned. Dog was glad all that intensity was over and felt relieved to have shared his secret with Bill. He would work out what he could do for his friend later, but, for now, he dropped to his knees. He was filled with sorrow, dismayed at the state of all his hard work. He placed his hands on the shell and once again tried to heal his pumpkin. He grunted and he moaned, but nothing mended. Bill shook his head sadly.

"I'm sorry, Dog. Don't think you are bringing this one back from the brink," he lamented empathetically.

Dog growled with frustration and sadness.

"I know, I know." He agreed. "This year we would've had it. It's all a mess."

Dog stood beside Bill, and they both looked dejectedly at the pumpkin.

"You've been here before." Bill put his arm around him. "There's always next year." Bill stepped forward and kicked the wooden pallet on the ground. "This is done," he said, overwrought by all that happened today. They both needed to focus on other things. "Come on, we've got work to do."

Dog stared at his pumpkin consumed by the grief for a dream that had died. As he had learned long ago, even with his incredible gift, nothing could be brought back once it was gone. That feeling of finality made it all the worse. He sadly patted his glorious gourd one last time, then slowly and reluctantly dragged himself behind Bill into the fields.

CHAPTER 13
Other Ideas

The sun was high in the sky as Dog and Bill kneeled in the dirt, pulling carrots from the soil, shaking the earth off of them, and placing them in buckets. They had been silent for a long while—both lost in their task and the whirlwind thoughts concerning their newly complicated lives. Dog was distracted by a solitary little white flower in the dirt and stopped to pick it up. He looked over his shoulder at Bill as he gave it a smell, then turned to the old man deciding to break the ice.

"Jessie?" he said hopefully. He missed her already and was hoping that she would come back soon.

Bill turned and saw the flower and gave a sad smile. "I know, it was nice having her around, but I don't think she'll be coming back," he said firmly. He knew enough about families to understand when you say things in the heat of the moment, those words can hurt and harm for a long while.

Dog grunted and shook his head.

"It's for the best." Bill shrugged.

Dog gently put the flower in a buttonhole on his overalls, and he looked at Bill with a frown.

"Family," he said pointedly and shook his head with disappointment then returned to his job of pulling carrots.

Bill stopped in his tracks and stared at him for a moment—that word rang like a church bell in the night. Bill took a deep breath then he also resumed his work. He wasn't ready to admit that perhaps there was something he could do to bring himself the true peace he had always longed for.

They continued their work in silence. Dog was fixated on his female friend; he knew she was in danger. Ed had promised to hurt her, and he was terrified. He knew she was tough, but he had to do something. Even though he had said to Pa that he wouldn't return to the woods, he had other ideas. This was life and death. As he worked through the field, a plan started to formulate. He looked at Bill out of the corner of his eye.

"Water?" he asked.

Bill didn't even look up. "There's some in the tractor."

Dog walked over to the tractor. He reached inside the driver's side window and pulled out a plastic bottle of water.

While watching Bill work, he had a drink, then slyly poured the rest out onto the ground.

He held the empty bottle up to Bill and called out, "Water!"

Bill looked over. "Go get some."

Dog climbed onto the tractor and drove toward the farmhouse.

Bill watched him go with a worried frown on his face. Dog was getting older, growing into his own opinions. *He had made a friend*, Bill thought. He smiled sadly to himself. He knew Ed was not the sort of person you'd want as an enemy. Fear started to grow within as these outside worlds were closing in around him. He didn't know what to do. So he pulled at the carrots harder and faster.

The tractor was parked outside the barn. Dog had finished filling up his bottle from an outdoor faucet, then walked over to the nearby truck. He looked out at the woods, then back at Bill working in the fields. Dog had always had a penchant for being sneaky, it was his nature. He liked secret cookie stashes and winning card games at all costs, but this decision had the potential to get him into all sorts of bad trouble.

He grumbled to himself, then put his hand in through the open driver-side window and switched on the headlights. The lights were barely noticeable in the daylight. He glanced back toward Bill, then casually walked to the passenger side of the truck.

Dog opened the door, fished around inside the cabin, found a pair of jumper cables, and quietly closed the door again. He walked into the barn and casually slid the jumper cables under his bed. He had remembered a time when Bill had had to drive into town to get a new car battery when the old one had died. Dog was gambling this same scenario would play out once more.

He promptly exited the barn, walked past the truck, and smirked to himself. "Snap."

Dog drove the tractor back to the outer field. As he and Bill continued with their work, the truck's headlights slowly became dimmer and dimmer.

Dusk arrived as Bill and Dog returned from the fields with a trailer full of carrots. Bill climbed off the tractor, while Dog dismounted from its trailer.

Bill noticed the barely visible truck lights immediately. "How'd that happen?"

Dog remained silent, trying to look as innocent as possible.

Bill climbed into the truck. He flipped down the sun visor retrieving the keys, then attempted to start the vehicle. The motor cranked but didn't kick over.

"Come on!" Bill cried, frustrated. They had a delivery first thing in the morning and this annoyance would put them behind schedule. Dog watched with interest as Bill tried over and over, but the truck failed to start. "Shoot," he groaned.

Bill leaned over to the passenger side and dug around, then sat back up and stuck his head out the window. "You seen the jumper cables?" he asked Dog. Dog shook his head. Bill frowned. "They should be in here somewhere. Check the back."

Dog obliged and looked into the truck's tray, then returned to the window. Bill was still fishing around the cabin. "No," said Dog.

"Go check the barn. I'll check the other car," Bill ordered.

Dog entered the barn, crouched down half-heartedly rifled through a set of drawers.

Bill stuck his head in through the front doors. "Any luck?" he asked.

"No," Dog said without turning around, his eyes wide. He was close.

Bill placed his hands on his hips and exhaled, "Well, I've got early deliveries tomorrow morning. I'll take the car into town now, pick up a new battery."

With his back still facing Bill, Dog smiled half joy, half guilty.

"Go ahead and load up the truck while I'm gone," Bill instructed.

Dog restored his poker face and turned to nod at Bill.

Dog watched Bill drive off while he loaded boxes from the barn, trying to display a scene of business as usual. As soon as the car disappeared from sight, Dog dropped his box, carrots spilled everywhere, and he started running toward the woods. He came to a stop as he passed his beloved cracked pumpkin with its oozing seeds. Sighing, he looked back to the barn and then toward the woods. With a grunt of determination, he took off at full speed.

Bill hurtled down the highway in his runabout toward town. His forehead was creased with thought. Business matters, enraged neighbors, and last minute changes to plans. He hoped Dog would load the truck and put away the machinery by himself. *By himself.* Then, he had an epiphany…

"Dog," he groaned. Furious that he had been so stupid. He slammed on the brakes coming to a full stop, then turned his car around with a screech and headed back to the farm, way above the speed limit.

Dog trekked through the woods in search of the female Sasquatch. He trained his ears, his eyes darted, looking for any movement, any clue. He called out, "ROOAAR," deep from his belly and throat. No response. He reached the flower-filled clearing from the previous night's encounter and tried again. "ROOAAR."

He waited a moment, but only heard the crickets in response. He whimpered to himself, then resumed his search, sniffing the air and walking deeper into the forest.

Bill's car pulled to a stop at the back of the farmhouse. He climbed out and scanned the farm. "Dog!" he called. He walked to the house and stuck his head in the back door. "You in there?"

He waited a moment but received no response, so he turned and looked at the barn. Bill stepped into the barn and looked around. He thought for a moment, then went directly to the bed, crouched down and looked under it. He pulled out a box revealing the missing jumper cables.

"Damn fool," he muttered.

He turned and spotted the long link of chain with a padlock wound around the thick column of the barn. His heart sank, he hadn't had to use that since Dog was a toddler, but this was an emergency. He hastily unwound the chain and hid the leg brace under the bed. He could play sneaky too. Bill stormed out of the barn toward the woods hoping to find Dog before trouble did.

The sun had almost set, but Dog continued his search for the female Sasquatch. He was scared that Ed may have caught her, or just as bad, she had roamed far into the woods, and he may never see her again.

He wandered out into a clearing and looked back from where he came, then he looked left and right. It was the same flower-filled clearing as before. He realized he'd been going around in circles. He whined miserably to himself.

There was a rustling in the bush. The hairs on the back of his neck stood on end as his heart flooded with a shot of hope. He sniffed the air… nothing.

"GRR! GRR!" he called.

An angry Bill emerged from the trees. He was holding a shotgun pointed toward the ground. Dog's face dropped from hope to despair.

Bill's eyes glowered with rage. "You have no idea what trouble you're in."

Dog took a few steps forward. "Lady," he pleaded to Bill.

Bill waved his arm at him to stop. "Don't move!" he barked.

Dog was shocked at the urgency in his voice and froze.

Bill quickly walked up to Dog, then used the barrel of his gun to clear shrubs on the ground before him. He revealed a fully loaded bear trap.

"I told you how dangerous it is out here, but you didn't listen," he growled.

Bill picked up a long sturdy branch from the ground and stabbed it into the trap. Its powerful steel jaws snapped shut in an instant. Dog recoiled in fright, seeing how that metal mouth could have caused serious damage.

Bill turned on him. "You disobeyed a direct order, you lied, and you cheated." Bill twisted and turned the branch until it broke free. "And you could have gotten yourself killed," his anger filled with the overwhelming fear of losing the one thing in the world he cared about.

Dog, looked wide-eyed and sad. He felt the old man's fear and understood. But surely Bill could understand why he did it.

"Lady," Dog said quietly.

"Don't be a fool. I said forget about her," Bill growled, in no mood to continue this conversation. He pointed with his stick, "Get back to the farm."

Dog hesitantly stood his ground. "Stay."

Bill's frustration at all that happened surged through his body. He raised the stick high in a threatening manner. "So help me, Dog, move yourself," he spat through gritted teeth.

Dog's posture stiffened with defiance. "LADY."

Bill had had enough. "Have it your way," he yelled.

He had never hit Dog before and he knew that this was not right. But he couldn't stop himself. He was scared of losing Dog. He was out of options. Bill swung the stick, but Dog grabbed his arm mid-flight, stopping it cold.

"FAMILY!" Dog roared angrily, surprised that the person he cared about most would try to hurt him. Bill winced from the pain of Dog's strong hand squeezing his arm.

"Let go, damn it," Bill gasped.

Dog bared his teeth and growled; his natural instinct came over him. He was not going to bend. He squeezed Bill's arm tighter and forced him to drop the stick. Bill's face fell, and he clutched his chest with his hand, panting for air. Dog was shocked and released his arm. Bill stumbled to a tree and leaned against it for support. Dog's anger melted.

"Pa?" he whispered.

Bill tried to catch his breath, but he was still fuming and definitely still scared. "Back to the barn!"

Dog was defeated. He couldn't find his friend, and he had hurt Pa really bad. He began to walk somberly and sadly back to Jackson Farm.

Bill followed behind, absolutely livid.

Bill escorted Dog into the barn. He turned on a light, and they sat on the bed together in silence. Bill looked at Dog out of the corner of his eye.

"I found where you hid the cables," he said as he got off the bed and kneeled on the floor looking under the bed.

Dog didn't say anything. He remained silent, feeling awful. Without a word, Bill pulled out the leg chain, and with one click, he secured the chain to Dog's ankle. Bill hurried to the barn door out of Dog's reach.

Dog shook his leg and tried to pull it off. "Pa!" he growled in anguish.

"It's too late for that," Bill lamented, then turned and walked out. Dog jumped up and ran to follow, but the chain snapped taught after several feet.

"PAAAAAAAAA!" he called after him distraught. He didn't want to be left alone.

Bill started to close the barn doors—he felt terrible, but he had to keep him safe. The day weighed on him like a mountain.

"Get some sleep," he said quietly.

He closed the doors all the way and secured it with a padlock from the outside.

Stoney-faced, Bill turned and stormed toward the farmhouse as Dog howled wildly in the barn.

Bill strode up to a pile of wood stacked neatly beside the house and pulled off the top log. He stood it upright on a large flat stump, then picked up an axe leaning against the pile—he was overloaded with emotions and had to let off some steam.

Bill raised the axe above his head and with great force, swung it down. *CHOP.* The wood split in two.

Dog continued to howl in the barn while Bill placed log after log onto the stump.

CHOP. CHOP. CHOP. CHOP.

Dog's cries were drowned out by Bill's aggressive chopping. He concentrated on nothing but the wood in front of him and the axe in his hand.

The chopping echoed across the fields.

Bill finally stopped in exhaustion. He stared at the barn doors listening for Dog, but heard nothing but his own heavy breathing. His chest clenched as he struggled to catch his breath. Bill stumbled to the porch steps and held tight onto the railing as he took a moment to steady himself. Bright lights clouded his vision, and it took every bit of his strength to not tumble over. After a few deep breaths, he continued up the steps and entered the front door, slamming it shut behind him.

Dog stared at the barn doors and wiped away his tears. He whimpered, feeling very sorry for himself indeed. He looked down at his ankle and kicked the chain around, grumbling under his breath. He looked at his shelf of shiny treasures and saw the picture of the trophy that had eluded him for so many years. His heart filled with sadness. His prize pumpkin was lost, Pa was furious at him, and the female Sasquatch was in danger.

Dog tugged at the chain dejectedly as he remembered a scene from *Los Pecados De Los Santos.* The great villain Hector Valez had been chained and imprisoned on an island by his evil identical twin who had assumed his identity and stolen his fortune. Hector had broken the chains and swam through shark-infested waters to return to his company and seize back control of his evil empire.

Dog looked once more at his shiny trophy. Hector had never given up and neither would he.

With renewed determination, he turned around and picked up the chain. With both hands, he pulled it, trying to snap the chain from the column. He grunted and pulled as hard as he could, but he gave up panting and out of breath.

He looked around. His face lit up when he spotted a shovel leaning against the barn wall. He went to retrieve it, but his chain stopped him an arm's-length away. He laid down on the floor and used the length of his body to reach the shovel, his fingertips just managing to grab hold of the blade.

With the shovel now in his possession, Dog stood up and straightened a length of his chain along the floor. Then, with two hands, he held the shovel by the wooden shaft and lined up the blade with the chain.

In one mighty blow, he drove the shovel down in an attempt to break the chain, but the shaft snapped where it met the blade and the chain remained undamaged. Disappointed, Dog threw the shovel aside.

He looked around the barn and saw the chainsaw Ed had returned hanging from the barn wall. He went to get it, but again fell a few feet short. He growled in frustration.

Dog retrieved the broken shovel, then returned to the chainsaw and used the splintered end of the shovel to carefully lift it from its hook. He was extremely pleased with himself.

He tossed the broken shovel, then grabbed the chainsaw's starter cord and gave it a mighty pull.

The chainsaw sputtered. Dog, now with a look of concern on his face, ripped the cord again and again, but with each pull the chainsaw failed to start.

He looked over to a shelf that had a large plastic bottle sitting on top with "2-Stroke" written in black marker on its side.

Dog retrieved the now useful broken shovel and tried to thread the splintered end through the bottle's handle. He managed to do so, but when he lifted the bottle, it slipped and fell to the floor, cracking and spilling all its fuel.

Dog growled and once again threw the shovel. Dejected, he dragged the chain over to his bed and kneeled on it while looking out the window. He looked at the damaged pumpkin and then toward the woods. He let out a small groan. He bet Hector Valez never had to contend with broken pumpkins, bear traps, and furious Pas.

CHAPTER 14
The Past is the Past

At nightfall, Bill was sitting on the lounge in the dark, staring blankly into the distance. His gaze dropped to the coffee table in front of him, where he saw the old VHS cassette labeled *Bill and Eleanor's Anniversary*. It sat directly in front of a picture of him and Eleanor. The day's events caught up with him—there was a weight that sat heavy on his chest. The guilt he felt having raised his hand at Dog, guilt at the way he had treated Ed. Sad after all these years it had come to this, and he was scared—scared for all of them.

Bill thought of Jessie, dear sweet Jessie. His daughter Mary and the pain that she had caused. How her husband had nearly lost them the farm and how all that stress had probably killed Eleanor. He recalled holding both of them as babies in this very room, marveling at the preciousness of life. How did he end up here? He knew precisely how. Each step. Each harsh word. Each *unsaid* word. Then he remembered Dog's word. *Family.*

He relived the fear he had felt when his body seized up in the woods and when he was chopping wood. He thought he was going to die. But he dismissed it as exhaustion. Just too much going on. But what if he had died? Died without making peace with Mary. Dear Lord, the thought seized him. Mary could die before him. He knew exactly what Eleanor would say to him right now—she would have a few brutal choice words. He smiled softly through the tears that he hadn't noticed had fallen.

Bill dug into his pocket and once again pulled out the hospital business card Jessie had given him. After examining it carefully, he took a deep breath then pushed himself out of the seat and walked to the door. He grabbed his jacket from the hook and scooped up his car keys from the table.

Dog heard Bill's boots crunching on the gravel outside. He sat up in his bed and peered out the window and watched curiously as Bill's car drove off. Dog grunted and laid back down. The Sasquatch returned to thoughts of his female friend as an awful knot twisted in his gut.

Bill walked through the hospital corridors, he stood in front of the door the nurse had pointed him to, Room 2. He took a deep breath. He had no plan, no speech—he was just there.

Jessie looked up and raised an eyebrow as Bill walked through the door. She knew how stubborn and fixed this old man was, but he did it. He came. Her heart flooded with joy as her face broke into a smile. She jumped up and ran to hug her grandfather. Mary turned her head weakly toward her father; there was a look of shock, then a smile of welcome through her pain and fatigue. Bill removed his hat and smiled uneasily back. He took his daughter in. My, she had aged—she was pale, and she was thin. His little girl was really sick. He sighed with relief that he put the past aside. This was far more important.

Moments later, after awkward pleasantries, Bill sat at his daughter's side.

As was Jessie's gift, she found a way to bring sunshine to the room and zeroed in on the happier days. She encouraged her grandfather and mother to share stories of life growing up on Jackson Farm. Soon they were all giggling in joy at the memories of Mary's childhood scrapes; beating up a boy who dared to try and kiss her, or Bill's four-year battle with a rogue raccoon.

"Tell me about Ducky Duddles," Jessie asked, remembering a childhood story about a pet the family had when her mother was a girl.

Bill roared with the memory of that crazy fowl. "Yes, yes, yes. That duck thought he was human, lived under her bed, refused to be with the other ducks. Was the most disobedient duck there ever was."

Mary and Jessie laughed.

"It was your mom's little baby. Followed her everywhere. Haven't thought about that blasted duck for years. He made a good baked dinner."

Bill and Mary laughed as they looked at each other. Bill had forgotten how he, Eleanor, and Mary had all shared a wicked sense of humor. A small wave of warm contentment washed over him as Jessie's eyes widened in horror.

"Seriously?" she gasped.

Bill shrugged with a smile. "That's life on the farm."

They sat in silence for a moment; the first moment of silence for a long while. Bill looked at his daughter. Though her eyes gleamed with delight, she looked tired.

"Speaking of which, I best get back there," he said softly as he stood up.

The emotion of the evening caught up on Mary. Tears rolled down her face. She had so much to say. "Thank you for coming, Pa. I'm... I'm…"

Pa cut her off. "It's okay. The past is the past. You just get well."

Jessie wiped away her own tears as Pa bent down and kissed his daughter on the forehead. His face winced in pain and he tried to catch his breath.

"Pa?" Jessie said with concern.

"It's nothing. Just… just heartburn," Bill waved her away even though he was unsteady on his feet.

"Doesn't look like just heartburn," said Mary as Jessie rushed to her grandfather's side and helped him sit down.

"I'm getting a doctor," she said as she dashed out of the room.

It was an hour or two later and Jessie was driving Bill's car while Bill sat next to her in the passenger's seat.

"You should have stayed for a proper examination," she chided. "I'm calling first thing to get you a proper appointment with Doctor Kennedy. If it's your heart like he suspects, then you shouldn't wait."

Bill gave a shrug. "Big fuss about nothing. It's just indigestion. I could have driven myself home."

Jessie had to laugh aloud. "You and mom really are as stubborn as each other."

"Well that makes three of us." he smiled.

They drove on in silence through the dark winding forest road.

"You know… I would never do anything to hurt Dog on purpose," Jessie said softly.

"I know." Bill nodded as the car returned to a peaceful silence.

After Pa was settled, Jessie made her way to the barn, unlocked, and opened the doors. She was holding a plate with a big piece of cooked steak on it. Still on the bed looking out at the woods, Dog became excited when he saw it was her.

"Jessie!" he cried as he slid off the bed and ran to meet her, but the chain pulled tight and tripped him over.

Jessie gasped and ran to his aid. "Are you okay?"

With her free hand, she helped him to his feet and walked him back to the bed. "Pa made this for you," she said as she placed the plate down on the side table and joined him on the bed.

Dog snorted and lifted his foot, showing Jessie the chain around his ankle.

"Yeah, he told me you're in trouble. He said Ed has laid traps, and he's trying to keep you safe."

Dog yanked at the chain. "Help," he moaned.

"I'm sorry, Dog... He made me promise I wouldn't take it off," she said, placing her hand on his leg. Dog let out a quiet whine.

Jessie frowned at the chains. "I hate seeing you like this," she said sadly.

Dog pointed out the window with urgency. "Lady" he said.

Jessie nodded sympathetically. "I know you want to see your friend. I'm sure you will soon."

He shook his head in frustration. "Danger!"

"I know. But we have to keep you safe. We don't know where she is, and we can't have you roaming the woods with Ed trying to catch you," Jessie said with a sad smile.

"NO," Dog said as he turned away frustrated. He grumbled as he looked out the window.

"I know you're angry at him," Jessie said softly, "but he cares so much for you... in his own way. And your friend, she's going to be all right." She looked out the window with a worried frown, hoping more than knowing.

Dog didn't respond. He felt Jessie's doubt, and he had a bad feeling, a real bad feeling that kept growing and growing. Jessie leaned against him and Dog put his arm around her, as they both stared out the window at the woods together.

By the time the moon had crawled across the sky and was shining high, Jessie had fallen asleep on Dog's shoulder. Dog, however, stayed awake, vigilantly staring out the window.

Jessie stirred and then woke. "What time is it?" she asked a little confused. "I should get to bed," she yawned. She stroked Dog's fur. "You should do the same."

Dog grunted softly but didn't take his eyes off the woods.

Jessie rose to her feet. "I'm staying on the farm tonight. I'll see you in the morning," she said as she walked out of the barn and closed the door behind her.

Dog snorted, then shuffled over to the side of the bed and picked up an old box of records from the floor. He flipped through them before placing one on the turntable. John Farnham's "Burn for You" began to play as he returned to his post at the window.

Nearly all the songs from Eleanor's collection of records were about love. Love being good, love being bad, and all the types of love in between. He thought about all those novellas he had watched since he was young. Every character had been motivated by love; it made them do crazy things, awful things, but, more often than not, wonderfully brave things.

He sat up straight as the realization hit him. He was in love. Love! He had known love in many ways. He loved shiny things, he loved Pa, he loved peanut butter and jelly sandwiches. He loved to make plants grow bigger and stronger, but the feelings he had for the female Sasquatch were different. He loved the female Sasquatch more than he had loved anything ever before.

All the lights on the farmhouse were turned off, and the full moon now cast a cool glow over the farm. Dog sighed as his heart ached to be with the one he loved. He maintained his vigil at the barn window. Night gave way to dawn as the first few rays of light illuminated Dog's alert face and the fields of Jackson Farm. A rooster crowed in the distance, greeting the morning.

Bill was dressed for the day and seated at the kitchen table, thumbing through a magazine while he drank a cup of coffee. Jessie shuffled into the kitchen wearing yesterday's clothes.

Bill looked up. "There's some hot water in the pot."

Jessie spooned some instant coffee into a mug, then poured the water and joined Bill at the table. She warmed her hands with the mug as she looked around the kitchen, realizing that nothing had changed since Grandma had died. The kitchen utensils were all in the same place, the various cozies she had crocheted still hanging around. All Grandma's postcards from her friends' world travels were still pinned to her corkboard on the wall. Jessie's eyes welled with tears, even a picture she had drawn for her grandparents in kindergarten was still stuck to the fridge door. Her grandmother had loved her so much, and she missed her dearly.

"Do you miss Grandma?" Jessie wondered aloud.

Bill looked up again and sighed as he rested his newspaper a little before responding.

"She was my best friend," he said solemnly.

Jessie gave him a sad look while she blew on her still steaming coffee.

He took a sip from the coffee cup, the one Eleanor had given him some birthdays ago. It had a crack in the lip, but he just couldn't bring himself to throw it out. Everything served to remind him of a life that he had once lived and never wanted to give up. Some days, Bill smiled; he remembered how much they had, and he was able to appreciate the blessings he had been given. Some days those reminders struck him like a truck, and he felt like he couldn't breathe because of the loneliness. Then the dark clouds would come, always the darkness. The betrayal of his daughter would well to the surface and bubble over, and all those memories caused a tailspin of emotions. But some days he was present, not held to the past. He was here now with his life, and on those days he felt the sunshine and tasted the sweetness, and he was okay.

Bill thought of Dog and knew that he was the main thing that had kept him anchored to the present. For that gift he would always be grateful. Yet he didn't know how to say those words aloud. He couldn't. The dam would break.

"Life goes on," Bill continued. "You get busy, other things fill your head. But you never forget."

Bill resumed reading his magazine, but he didn't really take anything in. Jessie watched him closely then finally took a sip from her cup as they both sat in the vast silence of memories.

The record had finished long ago and the needle crackled as the record continued to spin. The steak was still on the table next to Dog, untouched, hard, and cold.

Dog was slouched at the window; his fatigue had gotten the better of him, but it was only a light sleep. Dog's ears pricked up, hearing a loud howl echoed from the woods. A Sasquatch howl.

Dog immediately sat up straight and responded, "ROAR!"

He jumped off the bed. He knew what that roar meant, and his worst fears were being realized. He frantically started pulling the chain tied to the column.

The female howled again, and Dog turned to the window. He heard the panic, the fear in her voice. She needed him.

"ROAR!" he replied desperately. He wanted her to know that he was coming. And that he too was scared.

He released the chain and paced back and forth, growling and angrily swiping at anything within arm's reach. Boxes filled with knickknacks flew across the barn floor. He let out a tremendous roar in frustration.

Jessie and Bill were still seated in the kitchen when the ruckus began. They could hear both the female Sasquatch and Dog outside.

"What's going on out there?" Jessie exclaimed.

Bill threw down his newspaper and peered out the window. He knew full well what was going on. "It's that damn female Sasquatch. She's gone and got herself caught in one of Ed's traps."

Jessie stood up and rushed over to the kitchen door, "Oh my God. We have to go help her."

"Nothing we can do. Ed will see to that," Bill said in a low voice.

Jessie turned to Bill incredulously. They had to protect Dog, but she knew that it wasn't right to leave a Sasquatch out there at the mercy of Ed.

"If you don't do anything, Dog will never forgive you!" she exclaimed.

Bill kept his stony gaze on the farm outside. "Dog doesn't know what's best for him. He's angry now, but he'll get over it."

Jessie was furious now. "You're doing it again." She wanted to shake him.

Bill looked at her, confused.

"You tried controlling mom's life…" she started, her voice getting higher.

"And I was right about him," Bill started back.

Jessie stood firm. "It blew up in your face."

Bill's face turned red. "That's enough."

Jessie was not backing down. "Instead of protecting your daughter, you lost her."

"Jessie!" Bill cried. He was shocked at the sting of her words after the peace that had been made.

She calmed her voice; she knew attacking him would get her nowhere. He would just dig in his stubborn heels more. She looked her grandfather right in the eye. "Don't let the same thing happen with Dog!"

Her words hung in the air as the room fell silent. Bill looked out the window, frozen in the shock that numbs with words spoken true. He was too exhausted to fight or defend his position. He just sat there. Broken.

Jessie saw her grandfather in the light of reality. He looked older, weaker this morning. She saw a man who had fought for his country; a fight that had caused him to lose his innocence and trust in the good of the world. A man that had loved his family so much, but through cruel fate and his own stubbornness, had lost them. She saw a man that had filled that endlessly deep sadness of loss with Dog. That amazing creature had brought so much joy and wonder to his life, and now he knew that he was going to lose him too. She saw her grandfather for all he was, and her heart filled with compassion and love.

"You've got to let him live his life," she said tenderly. "Let him be a Sasquatch."

Bill turned to her, his eyes wide in the type of pain that comes with regrets, fear, and indescribable sadness.

Dog was still pacing the barn, kicking his ankle with the attached chain and angrily grumbling. He heard the female Sasquatch roar from the woods again. Her despair sounded worse, her roar faint and tired. Dog moaned in panic and sat on the bed. His heart pounded, adrenaline rushed through his whole body. He would no longer be caged. His anger surged. He thought of the female Sasquatch and his love for her. He thought of Ed and all the ways he had taunted him. His smashed pumpkin. Being too scared to go to the woods. The woods where he belonged. He used it all, every single memory of pain, anger, and fear, but also love. He could feel it flood from his head to his fingertips and toes.

He breathed deeply and gripped the chain in both hands near his ankle. He began to pull with all his might, harnessing those emotions. His face strained. The muscles on his back clenched. He threw his head back.

"ROOOOOOOAAAAAAR."

Jessie and Bill approached the barn, they had grabbed their jackets, and Bill was carrying his shotgun.

They froze in their tracks as Dog's roar shook the barn and passed through them like a trailer truck. Before they could register what was going on, Dog burst through the barn doors, splintering wood and smashing apart the outside lock.

Dog saw Bill holding a shotgun, he stood to his full height, bared his teeth and let out a savage growl.

Bill immediately lowered the barrel of his gun. He cautiously extended his hand to Dog, his eyes begging for forgiveness. He had never seen Dog like this. Never.

"It's okay, boy. I'm here to help you," he said with all his heart.

Dog continued to growl, the adrenaline coursing through his veins. He looked to Jessie for reassurance.

She nodded in agreement. "We both are," she said softly.

Bill looked at Dog with sorrowful eyes, "I should've never chained you up. I care so much about you. You're like a…"

It was as if Bill's heart and mind broke wide upon, "You are my son. I am so sorry," he said as he tipped his head in shame. He had treated him like an animal by chaining him up and had referred to him as an animal all his life. This amazing creature had shown him time and time again how special he was. He vowed never to call him Dog again. Ed had used that name to put him down and keep him in his place, and Bill could no longer abide by it.

Dog relaxed just a little. His eyes moistened as he looked down at the man he had looked up to his entire life, and he felt the truth and love in those words.

The female Sasquatch howled sorrowfully in the distance and the trio turned to the woods.

Bill stepped forward and reached to touch Dog's arm. "Son, let's go save your friend."

Dog smiled gratefully. "Pa!" he nodded.

Dog led the way as they all raced toward the woods.

CHAPTER 15
Out of Control

Dog, Bill, and Jessie were now deep into the woods surrounded by tall, dense trees. Dog sniffed the air and followed the female's howls as he moved quickly through the trees. Bill and Jessie struggled to keep up.

"Son, watch out. Ed's got the woods rigged," Bill shouted worriedly.

Dog grunted and kept running. His desire to help his love far outweighed his concern for his own personal safety.

A loud howl echoed through the trees, and Dog skidded to a stop allowing Bill and Jessie to catch up.

"Where is she?" Jessie asked.

Dog sniffed the air, then, without saying a word, dashed off in a new direction.

"Slow down, boy!" Bill called after him as he and Jessie continued to chase behind.

"I can't see him," Jessie panted.

A loud fizz sounded without warning, followed by a high-pitched whistle, which screamed from the top of the trees ahead. Bill and Jessie looked up to see a blaze of light rocket into the sky.

"What was that?" Jessie asked.

Bill's stomach lurched. "He's tripped a flare. Hurry!" he called over his shoulder to Jessie as he started to run.

They headed toward where the sound came from to discover Dog surrounded by smoke, looking up, mesmerized by the flare.

"'Son!" Bill cried incredulously.

"Shiny." Dog sighed.

Bill looked around with concern. "We don't have much time, Ed will be on his way."

The female Sasquatch let out another howl. Dog snapped out of his gaze and looked toward the sound, but Bill lunged and grabbed his arm before he could take off.

"Together this time, okay?" he said firmly.

"Okay." Dog nodded impatiently. He led Bill and Jessie a little slower through the woods, following the female's howls. He was frustrated by their pace, but he knew that Bill was right, they all needed to stay safe.

They pushed through a thicket of trees, and there was the female Sasquatch. She was trapped inside a net, writhing on the ground.

Her howl turned to whimpers when she saw Dog appear. Dog roared in anger and ran to her aid. He dropped to his knees, trying to rip the net open.

Bill stepped up behind him and placed his hand on his shoulder. "You'll never break through. I'll cut her free."

Jessie looked on in shock at the sight of the beautiful Sasquatch. Even in her unfortunate situation, she looked powerful and magnificent.

Bill pulled a knife from his pants pocket, flipped it open, then approached the female. She growled at him menacingly, and Bill stopped in his tracks. She had seen humans and knew they were dangerous and not to be trusted.

"Whoa there," he said, raising his palms.

She was feisty, to say the least, and he didn't know if he would get out unscathed, let alone alive if he went near her.

He turned to Dog. "You should do this."

Dog brought his face down to hers and hugged her through the net.

"Shhh," he whispered softly.

His voice soothed her, and she calmed down, trusting Dog implicitly.

Dog took the knife from Bill then, with one quick movement, he cut open the net. The female broke free and scrambled to her feet, snarling and growling at Bill and Jessie, who stepped back in fear. Her temperament abruptly changed as a shot of pain took over her face. She hobbled to Dog for support and whimpered in his arms.

"She's hurt," Jessie said quietly.

Bill looked up studying the tree, then the rope, and net. "She must have been suspended. The rope snapped. Looks like she took a nasty fall." He grimaced in empathy.

Dog helped her to a nearby tree and sat her against it.

Bill looked around nervously. "We need to get out of here."

"She may not be able to walk," Jessie observed. "I should check her leg."

"Ain't no way she'll let us near her," Bill said, shaking his head.

Jessie stepped forward anyway and edged as close as she dared to examine her leg, putting her nursing studies into action.

"I don't see bleeding or bone protrusion. I need a closer look," she said to Bill.

Bill nodded and leaned his gun against a nearby tree, then kneeled down several feet from the female Sasquatch and looked her in the eyes.

"You've had a rough morning, haven't you?" he said in his low gravelly tone, trying to be as soothing as possible.

Bill slowly removed a bottle of water, an apple, and a granola bar from his coat pockets, then tossed them over to her feet. He had taken a few moments to grab some snacks before they ran out of the house.

"I brought you something, you must be starving," he said with a smile.

Dog picked them up and handed her the apple. She devoured it in two bites. She then snatched the granola bar from Dog and tossed it into her mouth, wrapper and all. She chewed with a confused look on her face, then spat out the empty wrapper.

Dog guffawed slightly at how cute she was and handed her the open water bottle. She crushed it in her hand as the water spurted into her mouth and over her face.

Jessie smiled kindly at the female Sasquatch. "Dog, I need to examine her leg. Tell her I'm going to help," she said.

Dog waved Jessie over then held the female's hand. He grunted while giving her a reassuring nod.

Jessie kneeled by the female's leg. She spoke gently, "You're going to be okay. I just want to take a look."

The female had a look of uncertainty on her face but allowed Jessie to continue.

Jessie gently held the injured leg and felt it over, checking for breakages. She moved and twisted the leg observing mobility. The female winced.

"That's a girl," Jessie said as she stepped back. She turned to Bill. "I think she may have sprained it. She'll be okay, but she'll need to stay off it."

Bill nodded. "Dog, take her back to the farm. That's the only place she'll be safe for now."

Dog looked up at Bill gratefully. "Okay."

He put the female's arm around his shoulder and helped her up onto her good leg. She leaned on him for support, grimacing from the pain.

Thwack! Something whizzed through the air inches from the female Sasquatch's face and hit the tree. A tranquilizer dart sporting a tailpiece of bright red feathers was lodged in the trunk.

"You ain't going nowhere," Ed's voice rang through the woods.

Everyone turned in fright to see Ed, dressed in camo, step out from behind the trees. He pulled a new dart from a holster around his waist, slid it into his rifle, and snapped it shut.

Dog stood in front of the female shielding her from Ed while she still leaned on him for support. They both bared their teeth and growled low and menacingly at him.

Bill ran between Ed and the Sasquatches, holding his hands out for Ed not to fire.

"Whoa. Whoa. Easy there. Let's work this out," he urged. He was worried about all their safety, especially his neighbor's if Dog lost his temper.

Ed motioned for Bill to move out of his way with the barrel of his rifle.

"Bill, I'm darting one Sasquatch this morning and cashing my check this afternoon. You decide which one." He held the barrel pointed straight at them.

Bill tried to keep his voice calm, "Ed, my boy found himself a friend. I want you to leave them alone."

"Your boy?" Ed scoffed in disbelief. "Can you hear yourself? These things aren't human."

"Dog is more human than you," Jessie shot back, her temper rising.

Ed looked at Jessie with annoyance but remained silent. Bill took a step toward Ed. "Point it away, Ed," he demanded.

Ed kept his rifle locked and pointed. "I should have finished off Dog back when I shot his mama."

Dog exploded with a booming "ROOOAAAR!" He stepped toward Ed, ready to lunge and rip him from limb to limb. Bill turned urgently and raised his palm for Dog to stop.

"Stay there!" Bill ordered. He could feel this situation getting out of control, and he knew it wasn't going to end well.

Dog looked at Bill with confusion in his eyes. Bill felt the pang of guilt that had risen so many times whenever he thought of that day. He looked down. The innocent life lost. Dog had lost his mother and his rightful place to roam free in nature. He couldn't look him in the eyes.

"Pa?" Dog pleaded.

Bill shook his head in sorrow. "You didn't need to know. Nothing good would have come from it."

Jessie watched with sadness as she wiped away a tear.

Dog growled ferociously at Ed.

Ed aimed his rifle and laughed cruelly. "And your Pa, he just stood there and watched."

Dog looked at Bill with horror in his eyes. Bill turned his head, yelling at Ed over his shoulder, "Shut it, Ed!"

Bill turned back to Dog, putting both hands on his shoulders and looked him in the eyes.

"Son. There was nothing I could have done to save your mom. It happened so quick. But what I did do is take you home, and I took care of you. I loved you like my child. You're my son, and I'll do anything to make sure nothing ever happens to you."

Ed's eyes widened in disgust. "Jesus, Bill, look what you've become. It's nothing but a blasted animal."

Bill turned to Ed, his eyes raging. "Why don't you just—"

Without warning, Ed rifle-butted Bill in the forehead. Bill dropped to the ground out cold.

"PA!" Jessie screamed as she rushed to him.

Both Sasquatches roared viciously as Dog lunged toward Ed. Before Ed had an opportunity to flip his rifle barrel back around, Dog backhanded him, hard and fast, sending him flying against a tree. He too was knocked unconscious.

"Oh my God," Jessie wailed as Dog rushed to Bill's aid. The female leaned against a tree, growling uneasily.

As they helped Bill up, he nursed his bruised forehead. He appeared a little groggy. "Pa, are you okay?" Jessie asked, sounding worried.

"Where's Ed?" Bill queried with concern.

Jessie pointed over to Ed lying in the shrubs.

Bill's face flashed with fear. "What happened?"

"Dog hit him," Jessie stated, near tears. "Knocked him into the tree—I don't know if he's…"

Bill started to get up, but he struggled. Dog and Jessie helped him to his uneasy feet.

"I'll check on him," he said as he steadied himself, then picked up his shotgun that he had left leaning against the tree.

Bill surveyed the scene, he turned to Jessie. "Get her back to the farm."

Jessie's face crinkled with concern. "What about you?"

Bill shook his head. "I need to sort this mess out. Find out where the rest of the traps are." Bill waved her away. "Go on, keeping these two safe is our number one priority."

Jessie nodded.

Bill turned to Dog. "You too, boy, look after your friend."

Dog headed over to the female Sasquatch and put her arm over his shoulder. He turned to Bill. "Come?" he asked.

Bill gave him a smile. "I'll be home soon."

Dog was not happy about leaving Bill behind. "Come," he said more forcibly.

Bill shook his head and pointed. "Go on!"

Dog begrudgingly turned and headed off with the female, followed by Jessie.

Bill watched them go, filled with sadness and pride.

"Hey…" he called after them.

They both stopped and turned.

"No matter what happens, don't come back to the woods.

Understood?" he said firmly.

Dog and Jessie reluctantly nodded. Dog turned and continued walking with the female.

Jessie hesitated. "You be careful, Pa."

Bill nodded and waved her away with a half-smile. Jessie felt a sob rising, but she pushed it down. Now is not the time. He was an old soldier. If there was anyone that could look after themselves out here, it was her Pa. Jessie turned and ran to catch Dog and the female Sasquatch who had disappeared into the trees.

CHAPTER 16
Love

The trio had slowly made their way toward the farm, and the woods were now behind them. Dog, Jessie, and the female Sasquatch crossed the outer Jackson Farm fields and headed toward the farmhouse. The female was still in need of Dog's support as she hobbled along. Jessie looked back every now and then, hoping that Pa would come out of the woods, but at the same time fearful she would see Ed. All her fear and worry could not stop her from marveling at the two glorious creatures beside her. She had seen a few wonders of the world in her travels, but these two were out of this world.

"It's nice to finally meet your friend." She smiled at Dog.

Dog beamed back as he worked hard under the female's weight, but he then looked behind them with a great deal of anxiety.

They drew closer to the farmhouse and passed the pumpkin patch. The sight of his prize pumpkin split from top to bottom with its seeds spilled out was just another reminder of how Ed had turned his world upside down. They all stopped and looked at his pumpkin.

"Broke!" Dog explained glumly to Jessie.

Jessie nodded sadly. "I heard. I'm so sorry. Is there nothing you can do?"

"No," Dog snorted angrily as he nudged the female and they continued walking to the barn. Jessie swung the doors open. "Let her sit on the bed," she said.

The female Sasquatch sniffed the air as she looked around. This was the first time she had ever been inside a human dwelling, and the scent of Dog calmed her nerves. Dog helped her on the bed where she sat, intrigued by his shrine to all things shiny. She poked at his mirror ball and was transfixed by his glitter lava lamp and other trinkets.

Dog, meanwhile, paced back and forth near the window. He stopped and looked out worriedly at the woods.

Jessie, now seated on a crate, tried to console Dog. "He'll be okay," she said, but Dog could sense the fear in her voice. He continued pacing.

The female Sasquatch looked up from her curiosities and watched him for a moment sensing his unease. She grunted softly at him and stretched out her arm, which Dog took and joined her on the bed. She touched him on his chest and rested her head on his shoulder. The same energy that she could harness to make life grow flowed into Dog. His shoulders instantly dropped, his face calmed, and he placed his head on hers.

Jessie smiled sweetly and sadly. They all sat in silence.

Shadows shifted across the tree line as the sun passed overhead.

Bill stood leaning against a nearby tree with rifle in hand. He'd been watching over Ed for some time now, but Ed remained unmoving on the ground. He had thought about his friendship with Ed. How they'd never been really close, but had looked out for each other as neighbors.

They both knew that the other would be there if they needed anything. He was upset that he found himself where they were now, but he also knew his lies and deceit were to blame. Dog's safety and his life had always been far more important to him than any other human being.

Ed's eyes started to flicker, then opened. After a moment of confusion, he sat up and glared at Bill. Bill stood up straight but kept his rifle lowered.

"Now, Ed," he said calmly. "I don't want any trouble."

Ed eyed Bill's rifle. "You brought trouble into our lives, Bill," he growled angrily. Ed was a little shaky as he rose to his feet.

"Come on, Ed. We've been friends and neighbors for too long. Let's work this out," Bill pleaded, knowing that Ed was just as determined and stubborn as he was, if not more.

"You betrayed me," his voice raged as he looked left and right at the ground. "Where's my rifle?"

Bill's tone was forceful. "You'll get it back, as soon as we come to an agreement."

Ed spotted his rifle leaning against the tree behind Bill. He took a few steps toward it in an attempt to retrieve it. "I ain't losing my farm over some—" he spat.

Bill raised his gun at him. "Hold up," he ordered but pleading at the same time. He really did not want this to escalate.

Ed stopped in his tracks. His eyes went wide, surprised by Bill's threat. "You going to shoot me, Bill? You're no killer," he mocked.

Bill shook his head. "Don't be foolish, Ed."

Ed stood defiant, anger clouded his face.

"Curse you to hell, Bill Jackson," Ed screamed as he lunged at Bill and grabbed the barrel of his gun.

"Don't do this, Ed." Bill begged as they frantically wrestled for the rifle.

The morning sun was dazzling on dewdrops, but it did not provide much warmth at all. Dog, the female Sasquatch, and Jessie huddled together on the bed in silence.

BOOM!

A shotgun blast echoed from the woods. Everyone turned and looked out the window with pure dread as both Sasquatches growled uneasily.

"Pa!" Dog cried as he jumped to his feet and started for the doors.

Jessie sternly called out after him. "You can't go back."

Dog stopped. "Help!" he moaned.

Jessie shook her head. "He told us to stay here, no matter what." Her face crumpled in sadness. She nodded toward the female Sasquatch. "He wanted you to look after her."

Dog looked at his new friend with concern.

"Give him some more time. Okay?" she said softly.

Dog turned to look out at the woods again. This time, he spotted Ed in the distance, stepping through the trees. Anger fired through his whole body.

"ED!" he cried.

Jessie squinted as she looked out the window and saw him too. Her stomach dropped. Where was Pa? Her mind raced as her thoughts led her through the worst scenarios.

"Oh God!" she gasped.

Dog moved toward the barn doors. "Dog wait!" she cried, grabbing hold of his arm; she was so scared now.

"He'll capture you," she pleaded.

Dog looked at her with rage in his eyes. This was not the gentle, kind Dog she could ration with.

"Pa!" he replied with frustration.

"We don't know what's happened," Jessie pleaded, but the evidence did not bode well.

She pulled out her phone from her back pocket. "I'm going to call the police." This was now well beyond what they could all handle themselves.

Dog shook her hand free and was about to run, but Jessie grabbed him again. "Don't go. Let the police handle this. We need to hide," she begged, but she could see in his eyes he had made up his mind. She knew he was determined to protect himself and those he loved; there was nothing she could do to stop him.

"No," he said firmly as he broke free and ran out of the barn.

The female Sasquatch tried to jump to her feet but fell back in pain, and all she could do was howl after him. Jessie rushed to the window and watched Dog run to the fields. There was a heaviness in her whole body, and she could no longer hold back her tears.

Dog ran with determination past the barn and jumped over the surrounding picket fence. He headed in a straight line toward his one and only target.

Ed saw Dog approaching and smirked. He stopped walking to cock open his tranquilizer rifle and checked the chamber. He smiled and snapped it shut.

Ed looked through the rifle's scope and took aim, then pulled the trigger. The dart fired quietly from the chamber.

PFFT!

Dog yelped as the dart struck him in the chest. He skidded to a stop and pulled it out, looking at it with confusion and anger. He looked back at Ed and growled, then continued running toward him.

Ed remained calm. He cocked open the rifle barrel and slid in a new dart from his holster. He confidently raised his rifle again, narrowed his eyes, and waited for a clean shot. The gap between them began to close.

PFFT!

Dog was hit again, this time in the shoulder.

He stopped and pulled the dart out, angrily throwing it on the ground. His vision of Ed was now impaired as the double dose of drugs rapidly set in. He postured, clenched his fists then roared at Ed.

With only a hundred yards between them, Ed cocked opened the rifle and loaded another dart. He buried the rifle's stock into his shoulder and took aim, squaring up Dog in his scope.

Dog was unsteady on his feet, but growled while exchanging glances with Ed. He shook off the grogginess… then ran.

Seventy-five yards out.

Fifty yards.

Twenty-five.

Ed stayed locked on Dog. His finger began to squeeze the trigger when suddenly Dog stumbled and fell. He slid to a stop several feet before Ed. Ed smirked and lifted his finger from the trigger. He carefully approached Dog, still pointing his rifle and ready to shoot. Dog lay motionless, his massive frame slowly rose and fell with each breath. Ed kicked Dog's extended hand with his boot.

No response.

Ed gave Dog a second kick.

Still nothing.

Ed took a step back and lowered his gun.

He pulled out his mobile phone and a piece of paper from his pants pocket. He had trouble reading the small print, so he retrieved a pair of glasses from his shirt pocket. He dialed the number.

"Yeah. It's me… I got it. The Sasquatch," he exclaimed with a wild laugh to the person on the other end.

"He's alive. Tranquilized!"

"Probably another couple of hours. You bringing a truck?"

"I'm on Jackson Farm. That's right, the end of Patterson Road."

He looked at the hulking Sasquatch lying on the ground.

"Hurry," he ordered, then pocketed his phone and piece of paper.

"That was easy money. Your missus is next," he crowed venomously.

Ed noticed Dog's fingers begin to move. They dug into the ground, clenching the earth. A patch of luscious grass sprouted from the dirt around his fist.

"Still got a little fight?" Ed mumbled angrily.

He aimed his rifle at Dog but, to his surprise, the grass ran along the ground and started to grow around his feet.

"What the hell?" he stated, confused.

The grass sprouted thick green and sturdy vines that began to climb over Ed's boots. Ed lifted his feet, one after the other, snapping himself free; however, every time a free foot touched the ground, more vines regrew over his boot. Within moments, the vines had crept up his shins, and he could no longer lift his legs.

"What is this?" he scowled.

Dog stumbled onto his knees with one hand still placed firmly on the ground. He looked up at Ed. "Snap," he replied cunningly.

"Playing possum, hey?" spat Ed as he aimed his rifle at Dog, but the vines shot up over his body and restrained his arms. The rifle dropped to the ground.

"Let go!" Ed screamed as he struggled to break free, but he was helpless against the vines. The plant spread slowly, cocooning his body and had lifted his feet from the ground.

Dog slowly rose, but swayed on his feet. His vision was still blurry. He stepped up to Ed, growling and baring his teeth. Ed looked back with anger.

"Pa?" he demanded.

Ed laughed cruelly. "You're dead, you hear me? Dea—"

Dog angrily pressed his index finger against the vines circling Ed's torso. They restricted his breathing, robbing Ed of air.

"Pa?" he said again in a more menacing tone.

"Shot him. You're next," he muttered furiously.

Dog grabbed Ed by the throat and growled.

"I told Bill… told him you'd turn one day," he managed to gurgle.

Dog frowned as he considered Ed's words. He remembered his lessons at the dining room table, how Bill had warned him that too many lives were ruined by anger and violence. He knew Pa would want him to do the right thing. The Sasquatch, who had been raised as a human, overcame the deep urge, that primal instinct to protect himself and those he loved. He slowly released his hand from Ed's throat.

Ed gasped for air unrepentant and raging. "I'm gonna kill every last damn one of you—"

Dog roared and the vines grew around Ed's mouth, creating a gag. Ed struggled and screamed, but his cries were muffled.

Dog stood over Ed, breathing hard. He tried to control himself. He looked down at the man who had tormented him since he could remember, who had killed his own mother. He watched him writhe and squirm, trying to break free. He despised him. He fought every desire in his body to have his revenge.

Out the corner of his eye, he saw movement in the distant woods and turned to look. Through his hazy vision he could make out Bill as he stepped through the tree line. An overwhelming wave of relief enveloped him. He'd wrapped a makeshift sling around his shoulder and walked slowly, but otherwise, he seemed all right.

Dog swayed on his feet from the effect of the tranquilizer but was overcome with happiness. He yelled with excitement as he stumbled toward him.

The vines around Ed went slack and he thumped to the ground, but he was still restrained in a tangled mess.

Dog met Bill halfway and threw his arms around Bill in a loving embrace.

"Whoa! Easy there, big guy," Bill said with pure joy in his eyes.

He looked at him seriously. "You could have hurt him, Son, by God you had every reason in the world to harm him, but you didn't. I'm so proud of you, boy."

Dog nodded and smiled then looked at Bill's injury with concern. "Hurt!"

"It's just a scratch. I'll be fine." Bill dismissed.

Bill looked up at Dog's face again. He gazed tenderly into those warm brown eyes sprinkled with flecks of golden sun, and the sadness started to creep in.

He didn't want to lose him, because what else would he have left? His life had been focused on keeping him safe, protecting him from the world, and now he could no longer do that. The world was coming at them thick and fast. He saw that Dog longed for a world outside the farm, longed to know the world that he had lost, that he, his protector, had taken from him as a baby.

Bill knew he had to right this, even if it meant losing the most important thing in his life. He had to let him go, just like he had to let Eleanor go so she was free from her pain and aches. Dog would be free… free from his cage. The thought welled in his throat, and he could no longer stop the flood of emotions. He began to sob; he wept uncontrollably at the realization. The farm was his cage. He had locked him up. The most amazing beautiful creature that Bill had ever known existed, and he, William Jackson, had kept him caged.

Dog frowned. He was puzzled, he had never seen Pa so emotional; his heart ached for this human, this man, his father. He pulled him tight, he felt all his pain and sadness, and he shared it.

Bill buried himself into Dog's fur. He had not let him be who he was because of his own fear, because of his own loneliness. He wept for all that he had lost and all that he was about to lose. He wept for the years of anger that had kept him from his own daughter and how Dog had made him see the error of his way. He also wept for joy because he had been given this time with the most amazing creature God had ever created. And now it was time. Dog was ready; it was time to once again let go. He had done his job, and now he must go into the world.

He took a deep breath and looked back into Dog's face, which was crinkled with concern.

"You gotta go, boy. It's not safe for you here anymore," he said solemnly, trying to stop his sobs and tears.

Dog whined and shook his head. He was scared. He was confused. He was sad.

"Dog!" They stopped and turned. Jessie was walking with the female Sasquatch toward them. The female had a limp but seemed to be making her way better now. A big smile grew across his face.

He then looked back toward Bill and his face dropped again. Dog was unsteady on his feet, the effect of the tranquilizer and the emotions.

"Pa? No," whispered Dog. He couldn't believe that Pa was making him go. He looked back at Ed. He knew he was not safe now, his love was not safe.

"You can do this. You can do this!" Bill said proudly as he slapped him on the arms then pulled him close again. They hugged. Bill could feel the energy of the world in that hug. He felt at peace even though tears streamed down both their faces.

Bill looked up into Dog's eyes.

"You're ready, Son," he said determinedly.

Dog's heart skipped; he was leaving the farm, leaving all he had ever known. The fear was overwhelming but so was the excitement. He nodded.

"Love," Dog's faced swirled with happiness and sadness.

Bill choked up. "I love you too, Son. I love you too." When Eleanor had died, he didn't think that his heart would ever ache or break like that again. He had been wrong, very wrong.

They held each other as Jessie and the female Sasquatch walked up to meet them. Dog gave Jessie a hug as she wiped away her tears. Police sirens began to wail in the distance.

"It's time to go," Bill said, looking to the front of the farm anxiously.

Dog released Jessie and took the female Sasquatch by the hand. He turned to look at Bill with sadness in his eyes.

Bill pointed to the woods. "GO! Don't ever come back, you hear," he said sternly—his words filled with love and pride.

Dog drew a deep breath, his lungs filled with air. He threw his head back and howled to the sky. His joy, his sadness, his fear, his love—all of it rang out across the farm and the woods. The female threw her head back and joined him. Then, with his arm around her, they headed off into the woods.

"Look out for the traps," Jessie called after them as she put her own arm around Bill. They watched the two Sasquatches disappear in the woods. Their hearts wanted to break but fly at the same time.

A short while later, chaos had broken out on Jackson farm. An ambulance, police car, and a large truck with a cage on the back had all arrived and parked themselves outside the farmhouse.

Bill and Jessie were now seated on the steps of the back porch as a paramedic attended to his head wound courtesy of Ed's rifle butt. Bill's shoulder was bandaged and his arm was now in a proper sling.

Bill eyed the cage truck suspiciously, which was plastered with a sign that read *Sasquatch Research Academy*. He and Jessie exchanged poker-faced looks. They both knew to play it cool, very cool indeed.

Next to the ambulance, a police officer took notes as he spoke to a rotund, middle-aged, ponytailed man, who was talking animatedly in a low voice. The policeman nodded politely, but was thinking how he would rather help Mrs. Abbledean locate her lost garden gnome for the 15th time that year than deal with this.

Another two paramedics lifted Ed onto a stretcher into the back of the ambulance. He was tied down and thrashing furiously. "Listen to me! There's a Sasquatch! He lives here… on the farm!" he screamed.

The paramedics slammed the ambulance doors shut, silencing Ed.

Bill held his breath as he exchanged a quick worried glance with Jessie. He felt bad for his neighbor, but he had to protect Dog, and it seemed it would be at any cost.

Another police officer approached Bill and Jessie, while the paramedic treating Bill flipped closed her first aid kit and left.

"How you feeling?" said the portly officer kindly.

Bill and Jessie stood up.

"I'll be okay," Bill replied solemnly.

The police officer narrowed his eyes and spoke with a serious tone, "You sure you don't want to press charges, Bill?"

Bill sighed as he watched the ambulance drive away. He knew Dog was well on his way to being far away from here. Ed would calm down eventually. He just wanted this all to be over. He shook his head.

"Yes, I'm sure," Bill said quietly.

The police officer frowned with concern. "Well, you should at least file a restraining order," he offered.

Bill nodded, but it wasn't very convincing.

The police officer shrugged. "You let me know if there's anything else I can do for you, Bill."

Bill nodded again with a tired smile, and the police officer walked away.

Bill and Jessie watched the ambulance and police cars leave. The man from the Sasquatch Research Academy drove by slowly in his van and stared them down. Jessie sighed with relief when his van finally disappeared down the driveway and out of view.

They stood there and looked at each other. It was like they had been hit by a meteor, and Bill had no idea how he would ever heal that gaping hole. He was glad that Dog was safe, but he couldn't help thinking the worst—he knew he just had to keep going. That's all he could do. Bill shuffled over to the pumpkin patch and Jessie followed him. He looked frail and forlorn as they both stood side-by-side and stared at the broken pumpkin.

"He worked so hard year after year," Bill said quietly.

Jessie nodded. Bill smiled sadly and turned toward the woods.

"They'll be okay. She'll look after him out there," Jessie said softly, sensing his fear and concern.

"He won't be able to come back… ever," Bill said, the truth of the words weighing him down.

Jessie nodded sadly.

"He's a good boy," he said through eyes that welled with tears.

"The best," Jessie agreed, so sad for Pa.

Bill looked back at the broken pumpkin, he took it in. He remembered him sitting with it, his baby, day in and day out. Loving it, caring for it. He looked at the seeds spilled from its gut, then his eyes lit up. He stopped and picked up a handful of seeds from inside the pumpkin. Jessie raised a curious eyebrow as Bill beamed at her with a new sense of purpose.

CHAPTER 17
Peace

Jackson Farm was never the same after the fateful events of that late fall. Bill missed Dog with all his heart. They had been companions for many years and, like his loss of Eleanor, Bill took it real hard. Not a day passed when Bill had not thought of Dog. He always wondered about him, worried about him, and wished he knew if he was all right. He suspected he was, but he was curious to know how he had adapted to his new life given he had lived like a human for so long.

That empty space left room to create a new normal. Jessie and Mary soon became regular visitors; the pain that had congealed over so many years between father and daughter slowly melted away. It took a whole lot of tenderness and kindness which led to forgiveness, something that had never come easy for Bill. His experience with Dog had shown him how to let things go.

Somewhere in between all the bitterness and resentment, Bill and Mary both found a way to be there for each other. Together, father and daughter even visited Eleanor's gravesite, which was an immense step for both of them. They had all cried tears of happiness when they learned that Mary's treatment had been successful, and her body was now rid of cancer, but knew it would be some time before she was fully in the clear.

As for Ed, Bill never spoke to him again. Bill understood and wished he had done things differently, but he did what he did and, for him, that was that. Ed sold his farm for a good price, and Bill heard he had moved away to live with family in North Idaho. Colder and more isolated, which is how Ed liked it.

Bill's health never bounced back after Dog left. His body was tired, and he just didn't have the strength and endurance or even the desire to keep the farm going, so he decided that it was time to retire. He had worked hard all his life, and it was time that he learned to relax a bit. So, he sold all his equipment and let the fields grow long and tall. It suited him just fine.

He did, however, have one farm project that he wanted to see to completion. So on a fresh early summer morning, Bill started to dig and prepare the soil of the pumpkin patch. It felt good to work on the land again. It had been some months. He paused as the heat of the morning sun gave him a light sheen on his brow. He wiped it away with his sleeve and looked out to the field. He saw the tree stump in the distance. The stump that so many years ago had taught Dog that his gift couldn't fix everything.

He smiled sadly and surveyed his freshly tilled soil. Then, from his pocket, he pulled out a handful of seeds. *Prize pumpkin seeds,* he thought determinedly to himself. He slowly knelt down and planted the seeds, carefully, one by one. With each one, he gave the soil a loving pat, remembering how much care Dog took with each of his seeds, treating each one as precious as a baby. He vowed to do the same.

Every day for that summer, Bill would rise and tend to his pumpkin patch to ensure they had everything they needed to grow. And grow they did.

Every day, each little shoot crept determinedly toward the heavens. More and more rich green leaves unfurled, creating a tiny dense forest on the floor of the patch. Patiently, Bill would watch and tend with water and love. He had never in his life enjoyed gardening this much. It was so rewarding because he wasn't doing it for profit or for necessity. Instead, it was purely a gift, a task for its own purpose. For his son the Sasquatch.

Finally, the now luscious broad leaves sprouted golden flowers. The bees came and drank from the sweet nectar, and he waited with excitement to see what pollination would yield. Sure enough, with the delight of a child, Bill saw a burgeoning at the base of the vines. Pumpkins were forming.

With each day his pumpkins grew more and more. Big, full, and round. Bill proudly watered and fertilized, even giving them the occasional loving pat and song when no one was around. He would often stop during his work in the pumpkin patch and look to the woods, wondering, hoping. Bill ignored the wheeze in his breath, the occasional stumble in his step, and the tiredness that overcame him. He pressed on.

As the summer months perfectly morphed into early fall full of freshness and dew, he was relieved to experience a perfect seasonal transition. The pumpkin gods had smiled upon him. There was one pumpkin that had pulled ahead of the patch, and he concentrated all his efforts into this plump beauty.

It grew into a monster, wickedly large and weighty with a deep orange glow. Jessie and Mary who had been stopping by all summer were amazed at how big it was. Sadly, they could also see that Pa was slowly declining. It was getting harder for him each day to make his way to the patch. His gait was stooped and slower. His breathing even more labored. Jessie came every day to check on him and to help him work on his pumpkin; it held importance for them both.

By the time the earth was decidedly chillier, the pumpkin was complete. It stood gloriously, massive, and full. Bill couldn't have been prouder. With the help of Jessie, Mary, and some hired helpers, they carefully harnessed and put the pumpkin on the back of the truck. Then Jessie, Bill, and Mary all climbed into the truck—the County Fair was their next stop.

It was early evening a few days later, and the sky was already darkening. Bill slowly made his way through the tall grass of Jackson Farm to the back of the fields. He placed a shiny gold trophy on the tree stump. The trophy read *No. 1 Prize Pumpkin. Trinity County Fair*. Bill looked out to the woods with a melancholy smile. He had done it.

"Something shiny for you, boy. You deserve it," he called to the woods.

He wiped away a tear as he turned and walked back to the farmhouse.

After that Bill didn't get around much. They had to have a nurse come in daily while Jessie and Mary would also stop by as often as possible. Every morning they would set him up with a big comfy seat on the back porch. From there Bill had a direct view to the back of the farm, the woods, and the tree stump. He would peer through his binoculars to check, and every morning he would see the trophy sitting atop the tree stump in the distance. He would spend his days feeling the sun, listening to the wind, reading, and waiting. Waiting for whatever life would bring.

The season's paint themselves across the land in their glorious colors. On this particular fall morning, the sun shone bright and full over the farmhouse. The chill was still present, but the reds, browns, and oranges of the farm trees warmed Bill's heart. He had always loved the fall.

Bill was helped to his seat by Mary who tucked a blanket around his legs. He now had to wear a nasal cannula; he was frail, his pallor ashen and drawn.

Like he had done every morning for almost a year now he raised the binoculars to his eyes. This time his heart skipped with joy. The trophy was gone! In its place, growing from the middle of the stump, was a bunch of bright colored flowers, red and white and with a sprinkle of pink.

"Jessie! Mary! Come look," Bill called croakily as he smiled and wiped away a tear.

Mary squinted her eyes and could barely make out the stump and flowers. Bill was so profoundly happy, and he knew Dog was safe and well, that Dog was living the life he was meant to. Bill knew in that moment there was no greater privilege in life than seeing those you love become who they truly are. Even if it means you have to let them go. He got it now. There was nothing greater, nothing more powerful, nothing more magical.

Jessie emerged from the house holding a glass of lemonade. Bill looked up and smiled as he took the glass.

His voice was thin and weak, "He's okay, he's okay."

Jessie excitedly took the binoculars from him and looked out at the tree stump. She broke into a big smile.

Bill gasped slightly, he felt a pain seize his chest. The joy of his discovery was too much for his frail heart and body to handle. He whispered her name, "Eleanor." He had always hedged his bets. He didn't know what awaited him after his final breath; his last heartbeat. But if there was a god and an afterlife, she would be there.

He felt weighed to the ground by his whole body, yet he felt buoyed by life itself, as if he could fly. There was pain, but it was just his body. He was free. His heart seized one more time and took his breath away. His mind raced across his life, and the one thread that ran through it all was the feeling of a deep connection to each and every being he had known. It burrowed like thick ancient roots deep into the earth and then stretched like blinding rays of light to the clouds and space beyond. He didn't want to leave, but now it was his time. He could leave in peace. He had found his true peace.

He never exhaled. It all happened in an instant.

"That's so wonderful, I—" Jessie exclaimed.

The glass of lemonade rolled out of Bill's hand and hit the porch deck.

Jessie and her mother turned in alarm.

"Pa?" Jessie cried.

But Bill "Pa" Jackson was gone, like we all go. Gone in a wisp of tales, of joys and tragedies, celebrations, and heartbreaks, with all the other memories and mundanities woven in between. All we really leave behind is how we made people feel. All the other stuff—bank accounts and trinkets and treasures—will eventually be wasted away by the passage of time. But the feelings of those that have touched our lives are what we remember. And we leave our impression upon all those we touch long after our last breath, and our very last heartbeat.

Seed

CHAPTER 18
A Warm Glow

On that dazzling blue, cloudless fall morning, sixty miles somewhere north of Jackson Farm, there was a long trail of delicate flowers on the forest floor. Peculiar blooms for that time of year, petals of brilliant reds and yellows, which released a gentle fragrance that filled the air. The flowers sprouted behind the path made by two pairs of big hairy Sasquatch feet that were casually strolling along the forest floor.

Dog and his beloved were holding hands and slowly making their way farther north. She had adapted to some of his strange human habits like tidy caves, hand-holding, and no more chicken stealing. In turn, he had discarded his clothes long ago and rarely used words anymore though he was known to hum a John Farnham tune every now and again. His life on the farm seemed like a dream now, but the kind of dream that leaves a warm glow, and Dog carried that glow each and every day.

Dog and his love looked at each other and smiled. Just ahead of them was a toddler Sasquatch making her way confidently through the forest. She too was leaving a path of glorious little flowers behind her. Wisps of auburn curls framed the sweetest of faces, and her bright, curious deep amber eyes were a perfect blend of both her mother and father. In one of her chubby hands, she carried the pumpkin trophy. Dog smiled as his shiny treasure gleamed radiantly in the morning sun.

The chipmunks busily chattered, bees buzzed, and a hawk swooped and screeched across the morning as the little Sasquatch family disappeared into the forest.

A word from the Authors

Thank you so much for reading our book. As independent authors who self-publish, it's challenging to reach a large audience, so your support is appreciated.

To help spread the word and encourage others to read our books, please leave a review. It makes a big difference.

And if this is the first book from us that you've read, you may be interested in some of our other stories. You can find them on zealouscreative.com.

Kindest Regards,
Christine & Christopher Kezelos